KIBOGO

Selected works by Scholastique Mukasonga

KIBOGO

Scholastique Mukasonga

Translated by **Mark Polizzotti**

This edition first published in the
United Kingdom in 2023 by
Daunt Books Originals
83 Marylebone High Street
London W1U 4QW

I

This book has been selected to receive financial assistance from English PEN's
PEN Translates programme, supported by Arts Council England. English PEN
exists to promote literature and our understanding of it, to uphold writers'
freedoms around the world, to campaign against the persecution and
imprisonment of writers for stating their views, and to promote the friendly
co-operation of writers and the free exchange of ideas. www.englishpen.org

Supported using public funding by

ARTS COUNCIL
ENGLAND

A CIP catalogue record for this title is available from the British Library.

ISBN 978-1-914198-58-8

Typeset by Marsha Swan
Printed and bound by TJ Books Limited

www.dauntbookspublishing.co.uk

MIX
Paper from
responsible sources
FSC
www.fsc.org   FSC® C013056

RUZAGAYURA

Kamanzi, our sub-chief, came to take away our children. The Colonial had paid him to do it. He'd given him a watch, a pair of sunglasses, a bottle of port wine, two jerry cans of petrol, a swath of fabric for his wife and daughters. He took Gahutu's children, and Kagabo's, and Nahimana's, and many others. Even the ones who weren't ten yet. He brought them to the Colonial's field. So they could pick the flowers the Colonial had planted. Flowers with white petals and bright yellow hearts. The sub-chief had said:

'These flowers are for the war. They've told us Rwandans that we have to help with the war effort – the Belgian war, the English war, the German war, the war of all the White men. These flowers are medicine for the soldiers fighting the war. They kill off the mosquitos that attack them and give them malaria. We need many flowers. The Administrator said so to the chief, and the chief said so to me: that's why I need your children. We need children's small hands, the white Colonial said, to harvest small flowers.'

And the children harvested and harvested the flowers, in the sun and in the rain. The ones who went to school no longer went to school. They were picked up before sunrise and returned home after nightfall. They were too exhausted to eat. And they cried and cried, and they became ill, and when the mothers tried to hide their children, they came for the fathers, who got ibiboko, eight lashes.

That was when the chiefs turned pitiless. These were the Bazungu's chiefs. They had been to Nyanza, to a school for chiefs. They had shirts, trousers, sunglasses. They hobbled because the Administrator forced them to wear shoes. Behind them followed clerks who knew how to read and write better than they did and who recorded everything in their large notebooks. The chiefs were afraid of the abakarani, because they were the ones the Administrator invited on certain evenings to drink beer on his barza, and how can you hold your tongue when on top of that they offer you port wine, the ubuki of the Bazungu?

The chiefs went to Mass; you had to be baptised to become a chief. Everyone had followed their example: after them, everyone had received baptism; after them, everyone went to Mass; what else could we do but follow them? They went with the sub-chief to the parish assembly, the inama. As for the chiefs, they went to a spiritual retreat at Monsignor's house, the bishop's palace in Kabgayi.

But the chiefs were afraid of their white masters and their masters had told them:

'Now we're at war. We need men to dig the earth in the mines, we need a lot of iron and a lot of copper for our blacksmiths to make rifles and cannons. You have no idea of the riches you have here: there's Minétain, Somuki, Georouanda, and all the other companies that provide wealth for you and the Congo, where your men have gone off to work. It's up to Rwanda to feed them, and we need a lot of beans for the men who dig the earth in the mines. More men, and still more beans.'

And the chiefs had said to the sub-chiefs:

'I need men and I need beans, for if I don't find men, if I don't supply beans, they'll ruin me.'

And the sub-chief said to us:

'Men, beans and men, or I'll be let go.'

That's how the chiefs turned harsh and the sub-chiefs took the men and beans, and took away our children.

But not even the sub-chiefs were spared, nor were the farmers. Their cattle were taken, or else bought, but for a pittance. So the farmers hid the cattle; they sent herds to Bugesera, Kivu, Tanganyika. And when the Administrator asked, 'What happened to your cows?' they wailed and moaned and gripped their heads with their hands:

'What, don't you know? Woe is me! Woe is me! The tsetse fly and the plague decimated my herd. I do nothing all day but weep over Isiné, Rugaju, all my favourites.'

They slaughtered the last cattle: 'The Congolese eat only meat, raw meat,' the farmers were told.

As we know too well, one misfortune leads to another. And when the barns had been stripped clean, that's when Ruzagayura showed up.

Yes, that's when Ruzagayura, the great famine, came crashing down on the poor Rwandans, on the weakened men, the emaciated women, the sickly children. That year, the long dry season seemed never to want to end. We waited for the rain, which they say is Kibogo's rain, also called Bweramvura. We waited for it anxiously so we could plant the beans, peas, and sorghum. When it came, it was only to fool the farmers, for as soon as the beans and peas began to sprout, Bweramvura abandoned the hillside, abandoned all of Rwanda, and an even more crushing sun returned to parch our fields. We waited for the heavy rain, the one they call Zina; she came as if in a fury, spitting hail and lightning, then immediately left, content with the devastation she had wrought. The rain of Nyamvura, too feeble, could bring no aid. Dust had buried the now arid land under a layer of red ash.

Disease afflicted the potatoes and cassava that the Bazungu made us plant. They had said:

'With these vegetables, we can conquer famine. We shall save Rwanda, your country. Plant cassava and potatoes and they will save you from hunger.'

But diseases attacked the plantations. The potatoes were eaten away by rot and rapacious mushrooms, tormented by ravenous flies. And the cassava turned out to be poisonous. The barns remained empty. There was nothing left to eat but banana or fern roots, or wild grasses. We made a porridge out of dried banana leaves. Some people devoured the fruits of thorn bushes.

The infants were the first to perish, their mothers having no more milk. Children with great gaping eyes ate dirt, the elderly went off to die quietly, columns of families wandered the paths, vainly searching for scraps. Someone said, 'Over there, on that hill, they've still got food.' And the skeletal hordes started up and the vultures followed behind. Soon the path was lined with corpses. And those who survived found at the end of their road only empty barns and abandoned villages. And the sated vultures and hyenas didn't bother with their stacked bones.

Then the men, women, and children abandoned the hill-side. Entire families fled to the Congo. The country became sterile, desolate, deserted by both people and the Imana that provide abundant milk and honey.

Hope returned when Chief Kamanzi came to visit the hillside. His huge automobile that looked like a small truck caused the little children to scatter for their lives and the girls coming back from fetching water to drop their earthen jars, which shattered. The Swahili driver laughed at this. 'Our chief is here, he hasn't abandoned us, he's going to get us food.' Chief Kamanzi came with his clerk who always followed him around, his briefcase stuffed with papers, and with the sub-chief who had put on his trousers and shirt as if he were going to Mass. Everyone thought, *The car is filled with sacks of beans. We're saved!* But the driver took from the back of the car two jerry cans and three crates of Primus. The chief asked for large pitchers in which to pour the contents of the jerry cans. We realised it was sorghum beer.

Chief Kamanzi gathered the notables, the catechist, the sages, and the elders. Everyone squatted inside the cabaret hut around the large pitchers. Kamanzi wished the entire assembly peace. The clerk handed him a sheet of paper, for our chief knows how to read and even to write a little. He thrust it back irritably, then addressed the gathering.

'I have not come here to lie to you,' he said. 'May I poison our King Mutara if I were to do so! You all know,

8

and especially you elders, how many famines our Rwanda has known. But listen well to what I'm about to tell you: this Ruzagayura famine is not like the other famines. It has ravaged the entire country; it has bypassed not a single chiefdom, not a single sub-chiefdom, not a single hillside. It's as if it had a map of the country, like all the Whites do. It knows exactly where to go and it spares no one. So listen well and give me your full attention, for I am about to reveal to you a great secret. And this secret was told me by Bwana Ryckmans himself. You all know who Bwana Ryckmans is, he's the commander-in-chief in Usumbura. He commands all of Rwanda-Urundi, and especially, let us not forget, he is the godfather of our Mwami Mutara Rudahigwa. And this is what he told me: this Ruzagayura famine comes to us from Hitler, the chief of the Germans, who attacked the Belgians and the English, who attacked the whole world. And he attacked us too, us Rwandans, for he could find no other way to beat us than to sabotage the horizon by which the rain comes. He thought that famished Rwandans could no longer tend crops, that there would be no more men for portage or for the Congolese mines. And that the soldiers of every country fighting on the front would have nothing left to eat and nothing left to protect them from the mosquitos that bring malaria, and no more iron and copper to forge cannons and rifles. Hitler thought it would be easy for him to win the battle, but Hitler was wrong, for Bwana Ryckmans has brought

9

many trucks to the Congo, more than you can count, and he has recruited a whole army of drivers. They will come from the Congo to help us. They are loaded with sacks of flour, and rice, and beans. They are loaded with cassava, which cannot harm you. The trucks are coming, prepare your baskets to be filled. Bwana Ryckmans will save Rwanda.'

The people of the hillside clapped their hands as one must for a chief. The fat pitchers of sorghum beer and bottles of Primus were emptied as politeness requires. Everyone went to fetch their baskets and waited by the side of the path for the trucks to come. The trucks didn't come. Perhaps the hillside was on Ruzagayura's map but not on Bwana Rikamansi's. Others said under their breath that maybe Hitler had won the battle after all . . .

And then the priests arrived. At the main mission church and its outposts, this is what they preached:

'The sun, the rain, the clouds, the beans, the bananas, the squash, the sorghum, the millet, and even the cows, all of it was made by our Yezu. Isn't this what I taught you in catechism? All of it belongs to Him. He can do with it as He wishes. He gives rain when He pleases, and to whom He pleases: such is the merciful God. But if He does not give rain, it means He's angry. Perhaps He has reasons to be angry with you. And perhaps I can tell you some of His reasons. I know that you proclaim loudly that you've been baptised, that you are good Christians, that you are no longer pagans ignorant of the true God, but what do I see concealed under your medallions of Yezu and Maria? What are you trying to hide from me? Gris-gris that the witchdoctors made for you, that's what, with all their bric-a-brac of leopard claws, warthog tusks, snakeskins, rabbit bones, twisted roots, and feathers from those fortune-telling chickens that you don't dare eat even though you're dying of starvation! And you wear other things so shameful that I can't even name them. And I also know that you go in secret to consult the caster of spells because you wish evil upon your neighbour and, even worse, that you visit the poison seller to get rid of your hated rival! And do you think I don't know what you get up to on the hillside where the demon's grove still stands, which you've always been too afraid to cut down? You go to worship the devil beneath those cursed trees! And then I don't know what spirits possess you, what band of demons, but when they are inside you, when they have repossessed your souls that baptism had wrested from their grasp, you become like maniacs and your mouths foam with horrible blasphemies that would make you writhe in shame if you heard them in broad daylight.

'So now you know why Yezu is holding back the clouds, why He has denied you the rain. And your rainmakers, your abavubyi, and all their theatrics can do nothing about it. They can shake their fetishes all they like, shake the wands that they claim command the rain – Yezu has taken away their power, assuming they ever had any. Now, I tell you true, it's Yezu, it's Maria who will bring back the rain. It's they who command the clouds. We know what prayers are needed to bring back the rain. But we, the benevolent priests, we will not hide them from you, as the witch-doctors do their maledictions. You shall learn them at catechism and we shall recite them and we shall sing them together, every day of the week. And the young girls shall go pick flowers for the statue of Maria. Maria loves flowers and she has a merciful heart, she loves everyone, even black and ungrateful creatures like you. But on Sundays, you shall put Maria on the litter, the ingobyi, not the kind for the sick or the dead, but the one you reserve for brides, the one on which you carried your chiefs and your king before the Belgians gave them automobiles. You'll have to find youths who are still hale and hearty enough to bear her on their shoulders. We shall carry her throughout the hillside, in every field, every banana plantation, and you will sing the hymns that you have learned to bring the rain, and I shall walk in front of you and bless the enclosures and the fields and the plantations with the holy water of baptism, and we shall go to the top of the mountain, yes, all the way up Mount Runani, which your supersti-tion forbids you from climbing, but Maria will protect us and ward off the evil spirits and we will show her all the thirsting hillsides, the parched fields and plantations, and I shall bless the heavens, four times shall I bless the heavens, and if you pray, if you sing with all your heart, if you sincerely promise to renounce all of Satan's heathen practices (and you will have to come confess them all to me), then the rains will return.'

Not a word was said against the priest's sermon. Everyone was used to his reprimands, which rose and fell in harshness to suit the occasion. Anyway, these were just the bad manners of uneducated padri, and besides, everyone knew perfectly well that those who consulted witchdoctors would still go see them, that those who were initiated into Kubandwa would still get up in the small hours of the night to celebrate their worship. Regardless, we religiously followed the missionary's pious directives, which after all just might prove effective at triggering rain. The padri owned so many amazing things! And maybe it was their Yezu and Maria who had brought them all that. You never know!

At the parish assembly, the catechist designated the prayer teams that would take turns night and day at Maria's statue and entrusted twelve relatively healthy-looking girls with the honour of picking flowers for the statue, the last ones that Ruzagayura hadn't yet wilted. The relevant hymns were rehearsed endlessly by the women who would sing them in the procession. The catechist went to the mission to deliver his report to the priest; the latter, satisfied, announced that he would come the very next Sunday to lead the procession himself.

Meanwhile, we peered at the sky. Two boys who looked fairly solid were sent to climb a steep nearby hill to watch for the advent of the rainclouds. They waited in vain for the lightning and rumbles of thunder of the first tornado that would open a path in the sky for the rain. They came back dejected, saying that the same reddish fog was hovering over their entire area.

Then some began to mutter. Especially the old men, who said under their breath, 'All these misfortunes are the padri's fault. What are they doing here among us? Who told them they could come? We used to have a king, a mwami, and he commanded the rain, and if it wasn't him, it was the abavubyi, the rainmakers, and if the rain refused to come back, the wise men said to the mwami, "Relinquish the drum, you must drink the hydromel." And the king agreed to die and relinquished the drum to one of his young, hearty sons, and everything settled back to normal: the rain fell as it should, and the barns again overflowed with sorghum, beans, peas, millet, and taro, and the women bore handsome, vigorous boys – warriors! And calves filled the great courtyards of our enclosures. And if a rainmaker poisoned the clouds, we said to him, "You, umuvubyi, who has done you wrong? Leave us your vengeance, we'll exact it for you, don't take it out on Rwanda." And if the rain-maker persisted, we beat him until he set the clouds free. But these days, what does the king do? He's with the padri, the missionaries have locked him up to tell him about Yezu and Maria: they're going to baptise him, and for godfathers they've given him their monsignor who is in Kabgayi and the chief of the Belgians, Bwana Rikamansi, who is in Usumbura: the mwami has forgotten about his Rwanda. And the abavubyi, where are the abavubyi? The Belgians have thrown them in prison. Our Imana have abandoned Rwanda. Whatever can we do?'

There were five of them: five old men, the oldest on the hillside, sharing the last pitcher of sorghum beer at Karekezi's hut, when their host, having taken his turn to dip the communal straw in the last drop of precious liquid, spoke up:

'Are we to just keep lamenting? Are we to keep wondering who shall save us from Ruzagayura? Have you forgotten about Bajara? He was our sub-chief. He might know how to save us. The Belgians sent him away, and since then he has not emerged from his enclosure; he says that if he were to come out, he would be but a stranger in his own land. He has remained shut away with the few cows they left him and his five wives. They say he has more wives than cows. He has been humiliated. He doesn't wish to see anyone, he says that there are no more Rwandans in Rwanda, that they're all possessed by the spirits of the Bazungu. But if we went to see him, we'd tell him, "Bajara, you are mistaken: we elders are here, we are still Rwandans and we need you. You were once the chief on this hillside and we are all going to perish. You were a chief according to our customs, and you can do something for us, we know you can. Do not keep what you learned to yourself. You spent your youth at court, near the king, the queen mother, all those who hold the secrets that are the roots of Rwanda. The padri assure us they will save Rwanda. Could they be speaking the truth? Can their Yezu and his Mother bring back the rain? Will the rain obey them? We have no idea. But you, Bajara, we know that you of all people can come to our aid. The people are going to die: you have to save the people who are dying." That is what I would say to Bajara.'

The sages nodded in approval at Karekezi's words. They immediately decided to go visit Bajara as a delegation representing the entire hillside. At first the old recluse refused to see them: 'Let me die in peace,' he told them through a servant, 'I want to die with Rwanda.' They asked one of his wives, whom curiosity had drawn to the gate of the enclosure, to intercede on their behalf. 'What do you want from him?' she asked. 'You know very well he has nothing more to give you. We too are dying of hunger. Let us die in peace, and if it's the Bazungu who have sent you, do not set foot in this enclosure; do not add shame to our misfortune.' Karekezi replied: 'I know who you are, you are Mujawabo,

I know that you are his favourite. We wish him no harm. It wasn't the Bazungu who sent us. Bajara knows many secrets. He can help us save the hillside. He was once our chief. He owes us that much. Go relate everything I've just told you. You are his wife, you'll know what to say to him.'

They waited a long time, without daring to enter the compound. Finally, Mujawabo came back toward them. 'Bajara refuses to see you,' she said. 'He says that from now on, only death can enter. Moreover, she is already there, at the edge of his mat. This is what Bajara said. He wishes to speak only with death. He can do nothing more for you. Where were you when the Belgians humiliated him? But he has nonetheless consented to give you one last counsel. There is someone on the hillside who might be able to save you. Someone you have forgotten. Someone you have thrown into the bottomless pit of oblivion. There are so many things the padri require you to forget. You have lost your memory, the spirits of your ancestors have abandoned you. And yet, there is on your hillside a woman who might be able to speak to the clouds and convince the rain to take pity on you. She was the bride of the one who sacrificed himself so that the rains would return, the one whom the clouds took in. Those are Bajara's words, I'm relating them to you exactly as he told me: "Forget your Maria for now and listen to what this woman tells you. Do what she says and the rains will return."'

The self-proclaimed delegates were disappointed not only with the welcome their former sub-chief had given them but especially with his advice. How could Bajara possibly send them, the wise men of the hillside, to consult a woman? And what a woman! The one the entire hillside mockingly called Mrs Kibogo because she had refused all the husbands who had been offered her. The story of Kibogo was a children's fairytale. Even the last diehard pagans no longer believed in it. Or rather, had forgotten it. It was one of those pagan tales that the padri had decreed should be expunged. And yet, certain priests jotted it down in their notebooks. They heard it from the old men who were willing to tell these stories. The old men got the stories a bit muddled.

'We're preserving your nocturnal tales,' the priests said, 'for your children and especially your grandchildren, for the day when they're advanced, civilised, literate. Then we'll explain to them what your tales really meant, which you were unable to understand because they announced our coming to reveal the true God. Your grandchildren will be able to read those tales without believing in them. Whereas you, who have barely been freed from the bonds of Satan, still more than half-believe in the witchdoctors' twaddle. First you have to forget all that and listen only to the story of the true God. That's the only story for you!'

'But I,' Karekezi murmured, 'have not forgotten the story of Kibogo, and neither have you if you can open the gates of your memory. Our memory runs very deep! Remember: Kibogo was the son of a king, I don't remember the king's name . . .'

'It was Ndahiro,' prompted Gatoke, 'a king from very long ago.'

'That's it!' Karekezi continued, 'Kibogo, son of Ndahiro. And Ndahiro, the king, was very ill.'

'His eye,' Gasore cut in, 'his eye was hanging out of its socket . . .'

'Yes, his eye, it was the misfortune that had befallen Rwanda. And the land suffered from a great drought, just like today. And the rainmakers of Rwanda were powerless . . . The rain laughed at them, it refused to obey them. And so they went to seek out a great soothsayer, far away, in Gisaka . . .'

'No, no, you don't remember a thing, it was much farther away than that, in Buha; Buha is the land of sooth-sayers, where the calabash gourds speak on their own,' Twari objected.

'In Buha, if that'll make you happy . . . The sages of Rwanda went to seek out the great soothsayer . . .'

'His name was Mpande,' said Gasana, 'I know what his name was, it was Mpande.'

'Yes, he was the most powerful of all the soothsayers: it was he, in fact, who decreed that to make the rains return they had to sacrifice one of the king's sons, and Kibogo was chosen . . .'

'No, you've got it all wrong,' Gasana interrupted. 'It was Kibogo who volunteered. He said, "I am the Saviour, I am an umutabazi, it's up to me to save Rwanda."'

'Fine,' grumbled Karekezi, visibly annoyed by such rudeness, 'on the day of the sacrifice, Kibogo climbed up the mountain, and even I know which mountain, it's in Gaseke, and moreover the people from there call it Akakibogo, Of-Kibogo.'

'Wherever did you come up with that?' exclaimed Gasana. 'The people from Gaseke never told you squat. What are you talking about? How can you say that Kibogo's mountain is over there? I think you're just afraid to admit that it's here, near us. It's our mountain, Mount Runani, that towers over us with its great horn. And you also know why the mountain is called that and why it's forbidden to climb to the top – of course, this is not something we'd tell the padri – it's because a man was struck by lightning there, and wherever a man gets struck by lightning, that place becomes forbidden, no one can go there any more. But here we know that the man chosen by the thunder – I'm not teaching you anything new, you know very well, like everyone else around here, that it was Kibogo.'

'Yes, you're right, it was our mountain that Kibogo climbed all the way to its great horn. He had taken his spear, and his bow and arrows. His wife and children came with him . . .'

'And his retinue,' Gasore completed. 'Kibogo was a prince, and a prince never travels without his retinue and his cows . . .'

'Fine, fine,' Karekezi resumed, increasingly irritated, 'Kibogo and all his people reached the summit and all of them sat on the grass of the mountaintop and Kibogo climbed onto the boulder at the very crest that overlooks the void and was about to jump. Then the sky darkened, the clouds descended to Earth, and a small cloud detached itself from the mass and carried off Kibogo, his wife, his sons, his retinue, and his cows. And that is how Kibogo rose to heaven.'

'No, no, no,' Gasana corrected him, 'I've already told you, and everyone here knows it: it was lightning that struck Kibogo up there on the boulder that looks like a cow's horn. That's why the mountain is called Runani.'

'Fine, have it your way . . . the cloud and the lightning' – Karekezi concluded, visibly exasperated – 'took Kibogo and carried him off to heaven and Kibogo rose to heaven. And the rains returned and began falling over all Rwanda and the country again knew abundance and the king's eye returned to its socket. Kibogo saved Rwanda. Now be in peace.'

'But Karekezi,' Gatoke resumed, 'you've forgotten the part that concerns us. And Gasana didn't tell the whole story. He didn't tell us what Kibogo asked before sacrificing himself and rising to heaven, so I, Gatoke, will tell you: Kibogo asked that a hut be dedicated to him in the king's compound. A young girl chosen from among my clan would be the attendant, and the last one to be chosen, as all of you know, was from our hillside: it's Mukamwezi, she who did not wish to marry because of Kibogo, whom the padri banished when they overthrew Musinga and whom they cursed when she returned to the hillside. She is the bride of Kibogo's spirit. He might have confided his secrets to her. Bajara is of good counsel: she's the one we must consult about the rain.'

Mukamwezi was in fact the last remaining pagan on the hillside. When still young, she had left her family for the court of King Yuhi Musinga to serve as priestess for a mysterious cult that most have now forgotten. She had been banished from the royal compound when King Musinga was deposed by the Belgians, the latter having been strongly prompted to do so by the monsignor, whose name was Classe. The new king had ceded to the missionaries the hillside where the huts of his father's palace rose, and there they had erected a great church dedicated to Christ the King. The 'pagan fetishes', as the padri called them, no longer had a place in the handsome stone building, not far away, where the enlightened sovereign would now reside. The sacred fire that supposedly had been burning since the days of Gihanga, the founding king, was snuffed out; the spears, smithy hammers, and sacred drums were stacked up haphazardly in a miserable shed. All their attendants, the ones they called the abiru, those who knew the secrets, were expelled; they were told: 'You are nothing but witchdoctors and charlatans. If you keep misleading the people, we'll throw you in jail or out of Rwanda.'

Mukamwezi was still young when she returned to the hillside. She was not unlovely. She could have found a husband without much difficulty, but she refused all the matches that her family proposed to her. In vain did they try explaining that her vow of chastity no longer had any purpose since she'd stopped practising her ritual function and that, in any case, girls who had returned to the bosom of the clan after fulfilling this honour before her had all been provided with husbands, which fulfilled their fondest wishes: no argument could sway Mukamwezi, who was determined to remain a virgin. They nicknamed her Isugi, the Virgin. When the old sub-chief had been dismissed and the entire hillside, following the new one's example, had converted and been baptised, only she had stubbornly refused to follow the Catechism, leading the mission fathers to anathematise her as a heathen and an obstinate witch.

And so, the self-appointed emissaries hastened to see Mukamwezi. She lived in a round adobe hut with a thatched roof. They found her squatting on a mat in the shade of a ficus, busy repairing a milk jug with fresh sap from the tree. The five visitors approached, slowly, cautiously. Mukamwezi pretended not to see them. They cleared their throats in chorus.

'Ewe, Mukamwezi, ewe,' ventured Gasana.

She turned her head.

'Mukamwezi,' said Karekezi, 'we've come to you, hear us, the entire hillside has sent us. We believe you can do something for us all.'

Mukamwezi slowly looked them up and down. She fixed her gaze on each of the men who maintained a respectful distance, and said:

'So, it's you, Karekezi, and you, Gasana, and you, Gasore, and you, Gatoke, and you, Twari. So, I have the honour to see before me all the notables, all the sages of the hillside! What do all these whiteheads want of me? I am not glad to see you here, stooped over like that. Wasn't it the padri who really sent you? Before them, are you still men? What do those hyenas want from me? To chase me from the hillside? I don't want to hear your lies!'

'Mukamwezi,' Karekezi continued, 'we wish you no harm. It's not the padri who have sent us, on the contrary. You must know about the great famine that has befallen our hillside and our entire country. On the hillside, children, elders like us have died, mothers have no more milk, men have no more strength, the young have lost their vigour. Cows bellow at watering troughs that have run dry.

We chew on the last remaining roots. We are all going to perish. But you, perhaps . . . they said . . . maybe you could do something for us . . . they said that at the court, with Kibogo, you might have overheard things . . . the rain's secrets . . . the ones people knew when Rwanda was still Rwanda . . .'

'And your Yezu, your Maria, what have they done for you?'

'How can we possibly know? Perhaps they'll save us . . . perhaps they've decided our ruin. We don't know. Those Imana are the Bazungu's, how can we know? But we thought maybe you . . .'

Mukamwezi remained silent a long while, then asked abruptly:

'So, you elders, you wise men, what do you want from me?'

'Mukamwezi,' said Karekezi in a hesitant voice, 'make the rains come back, maybe you can do that. We believe the clouds will answer your calls. You who are Muka-kibogo.'

'You believe I can command the rain?'

'Our hillside, our Rwanda must be saved, if you can . . .'

'Come back in two days and I'll let you know . . . maybe . . .'

On the appointed day, the five oldsters went back to Mukamwezi's. She was sitting at the entrance to her hut. She signalled them to come closer and covered her face with her hands. Her breath started coming in gasps. The five men thought they could hear her murmur words they didn't recognise. When she removed her hands, the gleam in her eyes made them step back.

'Hear me,' Mukamwezi said in a voice that seemed to originate deep within her entrails, 'Kibogo has spoken to me: he is willing, from the skies into which he has risen, to reveal to me what I need to know to convince the rains to return to our hillside and all the land. It will be the day after tomorrow, and I believe you shall have to climb with me to the top of the mountain to call the rain. That is where Kibogo will be waiting for me.'

'But,' Twari objected, 'you know very well that the mountain is Runani, where lightning struck. Who would dare set foot in the place that the fire of the heavens has chosen? And besides, the day after tomorrow is Sunday . . .'

'And I, Mukamwezi, tell you this: it's from Runani that we must call to the rain, and you elders know why. Do you think I'm unaware what you'll be doing that day? It's the day when the padri plans to go parading his statue throughout the hillside and all the people of the hillside will follow him and will lose the last of their strength. As for me, I tell you, come with me, all five of you, and only you five, I don't want any others, and we'll see who, between Kibogo and Maria, commands the rain; but make sure all of you are there, woe unto all of you if one of you is missing at sunrise, and we'll climb to the top of the mountain and Kibogo will tell me to summon the clouds, the thunder, the rain, and we shall call the clouds and thunder, and the rain will fall on our hillside and on all of Rwanda.'

'We'll be there, Mukamwezi, we'll be there, all five of us. We're still men: we'll gather up the last of our strength and we'll climb the mountain with you.'

'Then don't forget, you must bring with you the branch of a young ficus, and hydromel in a pot of the type called igicuba. We'll need all of that for the rain.'

'There's no more honey,' said Gatoke, 'so no more hydromel.'

'Go see Bashishi, he knows songs that charm the bees. If he hasn't forgotten them, he must still have a honeycomb left. For me, he'll give it to you. Let one of your daughters who's still a virgin bring me this honey. I'll prepare the hydromel as we used to prepare it for the mwami: that's what is needed to attract the rain.'

The elders promised to return with what the bride of Kibogo asked of them. Having sworn not to breathe a word of their plan, they each slipped furtively into their enclosures.

It was the deafening roar of the motorcycle and, in the dry season, a cloud of red dust that always announced the missionary's arrival on the hillside. Then the children barely had time to rush to meet it, to challenge the mechanical engine that huffed its way up the narrow path leading to the church outpost. The children cried, 'Ipikipiki! Padri Ipikipiki!' until the biker in his cassock halted on the yard that had been cleared in front of the small structure, the only brick construction on the hillside. But that day, the children were too weak and too ill to race the ipikipiki, and when the holy father dismounted, his robe, helmet, and long beard red with dust, his benediction to the half-starved population was met with a vague moan.

The priest, who had donned a chasuble embroidered with a gold monstrance, nonetheless managed to set in motion the semblance of a procession behind the palanquin on which they'd perched the statue of Maria.

The priest went to the head of the procession. He dipped his sprinkler into the gourd of holy water that the catechist held out to him and vigorously blessed the desiccated banana trees and the arid fields. The statue pitched and rocked on the bony shoulders of the four young men. The person in charge of the Children of Mary intoned the prescribed hymns and litanies, but received only a feeble murmur in response. The longer the procession covered the paths of the hillside, the more it began shedding stragglers and slowly unravelling, until, with one desertion after another, it was now down to a handful of men and, especially, exhausted women, babies on their backs with heads lolling, who limped, stumbled, wobbled on legs reduced to knotty twigs, held each other up, and finally collapsed beneath the frayed leaves of a banana tree or under that shadeless tree whose brilliant red flowers are the daughters of drought. Having reached the foot of the mountain, the padri gave up trying to climb it as planned. The few survivors accompanied him to the church outpost. He blessed them one last time before straddling his motorbike:

'I know what suffering you are enduring. At the mission, we already have so many refugees to feed that there's nothing more we can do for you but pray. But have faith in the help of Yezu and especially Maria, whose heart is good. I am certain she has heard your prayers, and she will answer them. She will soon bring back the rain.' The motorbike jerked forward with a thunderous growl and disappeared in a thick cloud of red dust.

It was well before dawn, and as discreetly as possible the five sages left their enclosures and met at the foot of the path that scaled the lower slopes of the mountain. Karekezi was carrying the igicuba pot and Twari a ficus branch. They waited for Mukamwezi, hidden behind a large boulder, taking turns to watch for her arrival. After a while, as day was beginning to break, Gasore finally said:

'She's not coming. That witch deceived us, she was just making fun of us and soon the entire hillside will know about it. Everyone will laugh at us and call us stupid old pagans and the catechist will go tell everything to the padri and the padri will expel us from the parish assembly until we've confessed our sin in front of everyone and made penance. Shame will fall on our white heads. Let's get out of here and go home before the sun gives us away and we're seen, dragging our sticks like shadows.'

'Hush,' said Gatoke, 'I see her, she didn't deceive us.'

Mukamwezi's silhouette floated and undulated in the grain of the dusty fog like a reflection in the flowing water of a river. At times her pale face seemed to drift away from the rest of her body and hover on the swirls of mist.

'That's not her,' said Twari, 'it's her umuzimu, her ghost, we're done for . . .'

Still, little by little, the hazy form grew more solid and soon they all recognised it as a flesh-and-blood Mukamwezi. They also realised that that pallid gleam emanating from her forehead and cheeks was caused by the kaolin makeup coating them.

'Here I am,' said Mukamwezi, 'and I see that your fear of the padri did not prevent you from coming. You are still Rwandans! Did you bring what's necessary?'

They showed her the tender ficus branch and the igicuba pot.

'I, too, have what's needed.'

And she showed them a small spear and a calabash half-filled with hydromel.

'This is what we need, the igicuba pot and the Inkuba spear, the Thunder-Spear. That's what we need to pierce the clouds.'

Under Mukamwezi's encouragements and mocking laughter, the five old men struggled their way up the mountainside. In the most difficult passages, they helped each other out, gave each other a push, clung to one another. Sometimes, short of breath and heart about to give out, one of them lay down by the side of the path:

'Leave me here,' he rasped to his companions, 'this is where I'll die, and you'll find my corpse on the way back, if the vultures haven't made off with my carcass.'

Mukamwezi asked the one carrying the gourd to pour a few drops of hydromel in the palm of her hand. She moistened the dying man's lips with it, whispering a few mysterious words in his ear. Apparently it restored the supposed moribund's strength and will to live.

The pilgrims painfully resumed their climb. They huffed and puffed in vain behind Mukamwezi, whose feet skimmed over the stones of a dry riverbed, while the boulders seemed to bow down or melt away before her to let her pass.

Mukamwezi stopped to wait for them and egged on the ancients as they clung to the slope:

'Come on, now, stop dragging your feet like slugs. Remember that Kibogo rose into the sky like a prince. Kibogo is still a prince. We mustn't keep a prince waiting.'

The sun was rising in a halo of mist when they reached the summit. Mukamwezi pointed to a rocky promontory, the one they called the 'horn' of the mountain, which from a dizzying cliff overlooked the mottled hills in the mist. The elders crept forward, trembling, to the edge of that balcony that hung in awfully precarious balance.

Mukamwezi encouraged them:

'Don't be afraid, be brave! This is where you must call to the rain. This is where Kibogo rose into the sky to look for the rain. It is here, if he so wills it, that he will bestow on us a flock of clouds.'

Following Mukamwezi's instructions, the hydromel in the gourd was decanted into the igicuba pot, then she grasped the umuvumu branch, dipped it into the hydromel, and sprinkled it toward each of the four points of the horizon, saying:

I call upon the rains to fall on Rwanda.
I have come to conquer the drought.
I call upon the rain Bweramvura.
I call upon the rain Ndoha.
I call upon the rain Nyabuhe.
I call upon the rain Zina.
I call upon the rain Nyamvura.

She held out the leafy branch to the five wise men who sprinkled four times toward the four points of the horizon and recited the same incantations as had Mukamwezi.

The latter took up the small thunder-spear, rushed to the narrow promontory, and began dancing at the edge of the abyss, chanting:

I pierce the clouds.
Thunder, pierce the clouds.
Thunder, lead the flock of clouds.
Thunder, make the rains stream over Rwanda.
Abundance! Abundance! Abundance!

But at that point, it was no longer Mukamwezi leaping about the suspended rock. It was no longer a woman leaping about at the edge of the abyss and in the void: it was a lion, a lion whose roar was louder than thunder. And beneath its great mane that shone like the sun, there was not the muzzle of a lion, but the face of Mukamwezi.

The five old men yanked her back just as she seemed about to jump into the void, as if searching for the clouds behind the reddish droplets of the mist. They dragged her away from the rocky spur and laid her down, panting, her eyes rolling in their sockets and red as hot coals, on the gentle slope of the summit. After a long while, coming to, she said:

'I saw the rain. It spoke to me. I saw Kibogo in his cloud. He was waiting for me. He was there, right nearby. He was waiting for me. For me, his bride, he whispered in my ear: "I will free the rain." Why did you pull me back? Now I don't know if it will come, I couldn't go out in front to guide it, as Kibogo asked me to.'

'Yes, yes, it will,' the old men said, 'you woke the rain, you saw it, it will come, you heard Kibogo's promise.'

They helped Mukamwezi to her feet and held her up as best they could. They made her drink the last sip of hydromel that remained in the bottom of the igicuba pot and she seemed to regain her strength.

'We have to hurry,' said Karekezi, 'we have to return to our homes while the whole hillside is still in the procession. If they saw us come down from the mountain, there will be those who ask what we were doing up here and others who will guess what we did or will imagine still worse.'

They retraced their path. When they'd gone halfway, Mukamwezi ran down the slope, leaving the five old men far behind. She disappeared from sight behind the large boulder where they had waited for her.

The five old sages were able to return home without being seen, and the next day, when someone said to them:

'Hey, you, you weren't in the procession. I didn't see you there.'

They answered:

'Look at me, do you see these old bones? They're all I have left to climb up to death. How could I have dragged my old skeleton behind Maria? She can't possibly hold it against me!'

Needless to say, no one believed them. And an innocent child said in a loud voice:

'I saw you, Grandpa, you were with Twari, and Gasana, and Gasore, and Gatoke. And you were dancing on the mountain behind the pagan, behind Crazy Mukamwezi. You grandpas were all dancing, you forgot to be old, I recognised each one of you.'

The rains were long in coming. Ruzagayura persisted in burying the emaciated bodies under his shroud of red dust. But the tornado finally went on a rampage, conquered Ruzagayura, and stretched behind her a long veil of rain that covered the hills. The children danced in the droplets, the leaves of the banana trees firmed up, everyone breathed in the good, heady smell of wet earth.

The rains had returned; they hadn't abandoned Rwanda! We had to sow, replant what we'd salvaged of seeds and cuttings. The inhabitants of the hillside summoned up their last strength, hoping that, along with the rain, men would finally come to help them.

A few days after the first rains, they heard the sound of the padri's sputtering motorbike. He immediately convened the population in front of the church outpost. They listened in silence to his long sermon, not even the unruliest dared budge, and the infants slept peacefully upon the warmth of maternal backs.

'Let us give thanks,' the padri began, 'and especially to Maria, who is so kind-hearted: she is the one who brought you back the rain, despite your sins that had angered her Son. For I have been told that, up there, on the mountaintop, some of you indulged in pagan charades to make the rain come. Those who went onto the mountain danced with the devil. Or perhaps, worse still, with a she-devil! They have committed a sin, a mortal sin! They will burn, if they do not confess their grievous fault, burn for all eternity in the flames of Hell. Ah, how can those accursed souls not know this? Now we must do penance for those of you who committed this sacrilege, but especially you must show your appreciation to the Queen of Heaven who forgave you and saved you. This is what she asks, and this is what I heard in her own voice while I celebrated Mass: "Tell them that I want my statue at the top of the mountain, where they left the pagan wood without daring to cut it down. Let them topple those trees of the devil and, in their place, let them erect my statue. Thus will they remember all that I have done for them, and I shall watch over the hillside and protect its inhabitants, who shall be like my own children. No longer will they have to fear Ruzagayura." This year, with the rain that Maria has

36

sent you, you will have a bountiful coffee harvest. You will share with your Good Mother the money you earn from the scales of the merchant who buys your coffee. There are beautiful statues at the mission store. If your gratitude to our Mother is as generous as it should be, I will choose for you the most beautiful of all the statues and we will place it at the top of that still-pagan mountain that – I can see it from here – seems to defy our holy chapel, and thus it shall be consecrated. Can you still not know? Rwanda has become a Christian kingdom. Yes, the king, your mwami, Mutara Rudahigwa, has received the holy water on his brow. His new name is Charles-Pierre-Léon. Rwanda has a Christian king, Rwanda is a Christian kingdom! Who would dare return to the filth of paganism?

'May the Christian mwami reign over Rwanda! May Yezu reign over Rwanda!'

The crowd clapped its hands and echoed the acclamations: 'Ganza umwami! Ganza Yezu! Long live the king! Long live Yezu!' And yet the statue of the Virgin, on which the padri had so insisted by order of Maria herself, was not erected and the trees of the sacred wood remained inviolate. The parish assembly asked the literate man on the hillside to write a letter for the missionary. The coffee harvest, the missive said, was not as bountiful as expected; the weighted scales of the Greek merchant had robbed the poor defenceless peasants; the few bills earned from all that effort had been spent on medicine from the dispensary to save the children whom Ruzagayura had so weakened that they were susceptible to every illness. The letter they had taken such pains to write received no reply.

Gatoke, Gasore, and Twari all died that same year. Some saw in this the vengeance of the padri's god, but given their advanced age, that rumour won little credence. To appease their spirits – the spirits of the dead are always in a vindictive mood – they discreetly erected for each of them, behind the banana trees in the rear court of their enclosure, a small hut devoted to the cult of their ancestors and offered sacrifices of several grains of sorghum or millet, and a small gourd of sorghum beer: the dead don't have much thirst or appetite. Karekezi and Gasana lived on. Having become the laughing stocks of the hillside, they no longer dared emerge from the shacks to which their daughters-in-law had relegated them and where they often forgot to bring them food. Still, sometimes, one of their granddaughters or great-granddaughters (they were no longer sure which) shared with them her sorghum porridge and waited a bit impatiently to take back her calabash, while they finished the endless story they insisted on telling.

Mukamwezi disappeared. It was thought that she was hiding out from fear of being thrown in jail for sorcery.

Some claimed she had taken refuge in Burundi, in the scrubland of Kumoso where people came from far away to consult her whenever the rain acted up. Others said she had crossed the Malagarazi River and its crocodile-infested marshes, that she had stayed a long time in Buha, the land of soothsayers. There she is said to have shared or extracted the secrets of a fortune teller named Inangona, or She-of-the-Crocodile. Some credited her with the rain's return and even claimed she had been lifted into the skies and rejoined Kibogo, her husband. It was a story whispered only after dark, for no one dared tell it aloud in broad daylight.

AKAYEZU

Now we must tell the story of Akayezu. Even though this is not really a story, it must be told . . .

It was the dry season that brought Akayezu. The dust had already reddened the banana leaves when they saw him emerge from the van that resupplied the Swahili's shop, the only one around at the time. He always wore an immaculate white robe and sandals. It was precisely that prestigious outfit that had won him one of the two places of honour next to the driver, shielded from the dust. The few passengers allowed to ride in the back of the van had to squeeze in between the crates of Primus or Fanta or hold tight above the tanks of palm oil or gasoline and sacks of coal. The driver rushed to pull out Akayezu's small satchel and handed it to him with great respect.

Already a band of children had come running and soon surrounded the traveller:

'Akayezu, Akayezu! Do you have the bread, did you bring bread for the children? You haven't forgotten the children . . .'

Akayezu gently pushed away the children who threatened, in the crush, to touch and soil his dazzling white robe. He raised his right hand, like the padri, to make the gesture of blessing and impressed two fingers on the shaved heads of several toddlers. He crossed the deserted market square, occasionally raising light whirls of dust.

A parade of small beggars and a few women followed him on the narrow path between the spurge hedges that surrounded the huts. The men, unemployed in that season, had formed a circle around a pitcher of beer and greeted him with a resounding:

'Wiriwe Akayezu! Come dip the straw with us.'

Akayezu replied in a serious tone, calling each by his Christian name. It was as if he were lifting his hand to add to his salutations (the gesture he had so often rehearsed, in the shower room, in front of the only mirror made available to the seminarians).

At the entrance to his parents' enclosure, he addressed the handful of children still trailing him:

'Tomorrow, as you know very well, beneath the tall trees on the hillside, you will have your bread. Go home now. Tomorrow, I said, beneath the tall tree.'

In the forecourt, he coughed to signal his presence, as politeness dictates. His mother and five sisters came running. He dodged the maternal embrace to remove his robe and hand it to his eldest sister.

'Mathilda, take good care of my cassock, it is my only one. I'll need it for tomorrow morning, spotless . . .'

Wearing blue shorts and a khaki shirt, he then submitted to the prolonged embraces and let his body be felt all over, as politesse dictates. The women rushed about, procuring the much-loved and much-admired son and brother all the food and drink that the love and affection of a mother and her daughters could procure for the family's only son. None of which is hard to imagine!

They asked Akayezu's father:

'What is your son still doing with the padri? He's been there so long: does he still have things to learn from the Bazungu? Will he never be a padri himself?'

'Soon, soon. He's learning things that I could never explain the way he explained them to me, theorologalogy, sommatomasi, and all of it in Latini, all in Latini . . .'

'Those are all Bazungu matters and I hope they don't make him crazy. I've known some who . . .'

'I named my son Akayezu, Little-Jesus, as if I'd always known . . .Yes, you'll see, one day he'll be a padri, and not just any padri, a great one, a monsignor like the one who lives in the bishop's palace in Kabgayi, a monsignor, I tell you . . . with an enormous crown, like our king Mutara.'

The next morning before sunrise, Akayezu put on his cassock that Mathilda had devoutly washed and ironed by the flickering light of the agatadowa, the small gas can. He climbed the hill to the top where a thick wood still rose, called the Kigabiro, which they said was the remains of a former enclosure where pagan rites had been cele-brated.This was why it was forbidden to cut down the tall trees. The children, who must have been waiting for him, followed after him, the smallest among them watched by their mothers or big sisters. Everyone looked to make sure Akayezu was holding the satchel that must have contained the two loaves of sliced bread that the seminarian had bought in Astrida when the van stopped to take on goods and passengers. Immaculata, the catechist, whose devotion to him was boundless, came along to help him distribute the pieces of bread without getting pawed. Another woman was carrying a folding chair on which the good seminarian might be seated. When the cortege reached the top of the hill, the sun triumphed over the dawn and lit the old trees.

Akayezu took his seat on the folding chair that Immaculata had taken care to wipe off with the hem of her robe. He greeted the crowd with a resounding:

'Dominus vobiscum.'

To which the children replied:

'Umukati! Umukati! Bread, bread!'

Immaculata bade the children and their guardians sit in a semi-circle. This was not done easily, as several intransigents among the bigger children refused to abandon the front row. Lengthy negotiations ensued with mothers who deemed that their offspring were poorly situated for the distribution. Akayezu had to intervene to soothe flaring tempers: he promised that, insofar as possible, everyone would receive a portion equal to all the others but that he couldn't guarantee there would be enough for everyone because each year the number of those following him grew larger and larger. Moreover, from now on, he would give of his bread only to those whom he was certain lived on the hillside: he couldn't give out bread to the entire commune, the entire province, all of Rwanda. He was not Yezu.

Akayezu slowly drew from his satchel the two loaves of bread, each one wrapped in a piece of paper, and placed them on a tray that Immaculata held out to him. He slowly unwrapped the paper coverings and counted the slices. There were twenty for each loaf, not counting the two crust ends. With Immaculata's help, Akayezu cut each slice in half: that made eighty portions from the two loaves. It was hardly enough to satisfy the whole crowd that had gathered on the hillside. Some would be disappointed. Some might turn violent. Akayezu hesitated and, wishing to delay the moment of distribution as long as he could, he launched into one of his usual interminable sermons. No one understood them, but they were fascinating because of all the strange words, probably French but also especially Latin, which made his discourse even more incomprehensible but imbued it with the mystery of a magic incantation.

Ultimately, he had to start giving out the bread, for impatient mutters and shouts were rising from the assembly. Two imposing matrons volunteered to surround and protect the baskets and those bearing them. Akayezu began dispensing: he took the slices one by one and placed them in the outstretched hands of the children and women. The smallest ones clung to his cassock and the mothers held out their babies to him at arm's length. But the oldest children who had been relegated to the back rows started pushing, shoving, knocking people over, trampling the children and mothers who were in their way. The matrons endeavoured with all their opulence to protect Akayezu and the baskets, but soon these human shields were themselves overcome. Akayezu tried one last time to repel the assault by shouting at the top of his lungs: '*Vade retro Shatani!*' but then he, the baskets, Immaculata, and the matrons disappeared in the fray. The big kids ran off, the pockets of their tattered shorts bulging with slices of bread. 'It's for my little sister who's sick!' one of them shouted.

Akayezu was left on his knees, his cassock red with dust, amid the bawling children and whimpering women. 'Cursed be the gluttonous,' he lamented, 'for they would snatch the celestial bread from the angels come to Earth and fight like dogs to grab the manna that God brought forth to nourish them during the great drought.'

But maybe things didn't always go as badly as all that. There has always been spiteful gossip on the hills, and no one could say for sure how many dry seasons Akayezu the seminarian was seen handing out his two loaves of bread to the children.

It was long wondered on the hillside why the missionaries had chosen Akayezu to study at the minor seminary in Kabgayi. Normally it was the sons of chiefs or catechists who got preference. And naturally, it was an extraordinary favour to be accepted as a minor seminarian. The minor seminary was the royal road, and more or less the only road, to the knowledge of the Whites. And if you were then among the chosen few who went on to the Saint Charles Borromeo major seminary in Nyakibanda, you might someday have the opportunity to become a padri, a real one, a member of the native clergy, almost the equal of the missionaries themselves. But it was also possible to diverge onto another path, which left you well positioned among the abakarani, the clerks who were feared by everyone, even by chiefs of high lineage who until then had counted on the incalculable number of their cows rather than on those papers the Europeans gave you if you went to their school, called diplomas. In any case, whether you came out of the minor or the major seminary, you belonged, as no one could deny, to the superior class of 'the advanced'.

Akayezu's father was not reputed to be a model Christian. They even said he'd long remained a pagan and had been among the last to get himself baptised. At Mass, he displayed only moderate fervour. He rarely attended the parish assembly. Perhaps it was to compensate for his lack of zeal that he had given his son (the only boy in a family that already counted five daughters) the name Akayezu, Little Jesus. His wife, a renowned storyteller, had more children at her evening gatherings than did the catechism classes. She would tell of the innumerable exploits of King Ruganzu Ndori, who with his magic arrows had made water spring from so many sources; of the sacrifices of all those who had given their lives to save Rwanda; of Queen Robwe, who had died by throwing herself onto the sacred drum of the enemy king; and of Kibogo, who, to conquer the drought, had been lifted into the firmament, at the top of the mountain of which the hillside seemed to be the last blip.

In grade school, Akayezu, who had been baptised with the name Theogenes, did not especially stand out. Like the other pupils, he was imperturbably well-behaved and attentive, as are all Rwandan schoolchildren. He ardently repeated the French words and phrases the instructor wrote on the chalkboard, carefully articulating each syllable. Like all the others, when the teacher asked a question, his hand shot up and he snapped his fingers with all his might. Even if he didn't know the answer: 'Ask me, teacher, ask me, teacher,' he begged with the rest of the class. But he was always beaten to it by Hakizimana or Butoyi, always the same two, to whom the teacher ultimately granted the privilege of answering.

But if you asked why the missionaries had chosen Akayezu for admission to the minor seminary, when there were so many others more deserving, and even sons of catechists and sons of chiefs and subchiefs, you were told: 'They chose Akayezu for Kabgayi because he was a little thief.' That made everybody laugh, and if you probed harder – 'What do you mean, a little thief?' – someone always ended up telling you the story of the 'vocation', as the padri called it, of Akayezu the big liar, a story like a children's fairy tale.

So, one day, when a padri was walking and reading in his big fat book, as is their custom, he spotted Akayezu coming toward him, his own nose plunged into a book that was bigger than he was. Akayezu tried to turn back and flee as fast as his legs would carry him while hiding the book under his shirt, but the book fell, Akayezu tripped over it, ended up splayed on the ground, and felt the padri's grip lifting him roughly by the nape of the neck.

'You little thief,' said the padri, 'pick up that book and give it to me, and be quick about it.'

Trembling mightily, Akayezu handed over the book.

'I knew it: it's Father Anselme's breviary. He thought he'd misplaced it, but how can you misplace a breviary! You're the one who took it, you little hoodlum! I can't imagine what you thought you'd do with it – don't you know you've committed a mortal sin?'

'I didn't steal it, I found it in the road, it fell out of the saddle bags of his pikipiki.'

'So why didn't you run to the church to give it back to him? You don't call that stealing?'

'I was going to give it back to him, but I wanted to read it first.'

'Read it?'

'Yes, I know the book tells the story of Yezu. My name is Theogenes, but my father gave me the name Yezu, I'm called Akayezu, so I wanted to know what the padri's book really says about Yezu. I don't think the catechist is telling us the whole story. I want to know everything about Yezu, I want to do everything like Yezu, since my father called me Akayezu.'

'So what did you learn from that book?'

'I didn't learn anything. It's not French in this book. It's your own language, your padri language. I don't understand it. And you don't want to teach it to us like French because it's your ibanga, your secret for just the padri.'

'So you want to learn Latin?'

'I want to do like you, padri, know everything you know. I want to do like Yezu in your book. He was powerful, and isn't my name Akayezu? It was my father who gave me that name: Akayezu. I don't want to steal your book, I just want to learn Latin to be able to read it and do like Yezu because my father named me Akayezu.'

The padri was touched by Akayezu's zeal:

'My boy,' he said, 'if you're good, if you do well in school, if you make progress, and especially if you pray every day to Yezu and Maria, I'll see to it that you get accepted into Kabgayi where you'll learn not only Latin but the language of the books where they tell the story of Yezu's life. And if you really want to be like Yezu, and if Yezu chooses you, you might even become a padri like me.'

And that, according to legend, is how Akayezu entered the minor seminary at Kabgayi.

Every year, during the three months of holiday that corresponded to the short dry season in Rwanda, Akayezu endeavoured, as he put it, to 'evangelise' his hillside. He visited each enclosure one by one, enquired anxiously about the health of the children, about the cows for the Tutsis, about the sorghum and corn harvests for the Hutus, and about the proper firing of pots for the Batwa. He blessed the calves and the newborns, the huts, the granaries, the fields, and the pitchers. A throng of children followed behind him, calling out, 'Akayezu! Akayezu!' Several women surrounded him at a respectful distance. Immaculata, the auxiliary catechist who taught the Gospel to the smallest children, was his main disciple. She and her companions tried to disperse the swarm of youngsters that pestered him like flies around a cow's muzzle.

On Sundays, Akayezu preached beneath the tall trees of Kigabiro. His sermons drew a sizeable crowd – not that they understood a thing of his Latin-studded speeches, but they flocked as if to see a rare spectacle that made many laugh, and that the children imitated. The latter had invented a kind of gibberish that supposedly mimicked the seminarian's language.

His preaching earned him harsh reprimands from the church fathers in the neighbouring mission, who complained that he was keeping the faithful from attending Sunday Mass, which is an obligation for all Christians.

They summoned him and told him in no uncertain terms that a simple minor seminarian did not have the right to preach without authorisation from the Father Superior of the minor seminary, or even the Bishop himself. The missionaries alerted the authorities in Kabgayi, who also grew concerned about their student's orthodoxy, and especially about his mental stability. Still, the incident went no further, as Akayezu renounced his grand public declamations and contented himself from then on with preaching discreetly in the thick shadows of the sacred wood for the few women who followed wherever he went.

No one understood what it was you did in a seminary. What could you possibly learn there that you hadn't already learned in catechism or from the instructor, and why did it take so long to become a padri? When Akayezu talked about the seminary, what he said was just as incomprehensible as those poems by ancient warriors that old people still recited at weddings and that everyone laughed at. The ancient warriors often boasted of imaginary exploits, and a few evil-tongued individuals suggested under their breath that it was no different for the seminarian, who claimed to share all the White man's knowledge.

The good seminarian tried with tireless patience and benevolence to answer the naïve or malicious questions asked him by the boldest souls or those who wanted to trip him up:

'So, Akayezu, do you eat Bazungu food? Tell us what the Whites eat. Doesn't it make you sick?'

A few old women who had lost all sense of shame asked:

'And has your poop turned white too?'

And others:

'I've heard you sleep all alone on a White man's bed. How can you sleep without someone next to you?'

And still others:

'The padri don't have wives, so tell us, where do the little padri come from? Is that why they've come to our village, to steal our boys?'

And those who remembered their catechism, especially the women, asked him:

'Akayezu, the padri tell us that Yezu rose to Heaven, but they've never told us how; since you'll be a padri someday, did they tell you?'

And Akayezu explained:

'They said a cloud came to gather Yezu, and he rose to Heaven on a cloud like his mama. I've seen Maria on the padri's images rising to Heaven on her cloud way above the rain; they also say, according to Saint Paul, that it's Yezu who will come back to gather all of us on a cloud.'

'But,' objected a scholar, 'the Whites have airplanes that go into the sky, I know this, I've seen them. Have they seen Yezu in the sky?'

'The sky of airplanes is not the same sky as Yezu's Heaven. Yezu's Heaven is the firmament: "Remember this well and look carefully at the clouds," the padri say, "and perhaps one day you will see Yezu reigning on his shining throne that will glide toward us, from cloud to cloud."'

'It's true that, among us,' an old woman remarked, 'they say Kibogo also rose into the firmament, like you say. They even tell that it happened at the top of our mountain. It's your own mother who tells that story. Is your mother lying?'

'Yes, you might be speaking the truth, for my mother never tells lies: Kibogo saved Rwanda, he rose to Heaven, but some say it was the lightning that carried him off.'

'And do you think Kibogo will ever return?'

'Perhaps, perhaps he'll return – if the drought attacks Rwanda again, if great misfortunes befall our Rwanda, who can say? Perhaps then he too will return in the clouds,' Akayezu answered so as not to offend the old granny.

Akayezu's reflections on the return of Kibogo reached the ears of the chief catechist and sent him into a rage: 'What Akayezu said were Satan's words. That's not what we're teaching him at the seminary and it's not what *I* teach those who follow my catechism. There's no mention of Kibogo in the book the priests gave me. Akayezu's words are lies inspired by the Great Liar. I'm going to tell all this to our fathers at the main mission and, believe me, they're already well aware of that impostor. He'd better not expect any absolution from them.' But the good people of the hillside continued to follow and listen to Akayezu in secret. The priests of the main mission gauged that it was better to wait before cutting him loose, as the statements reported by the chief catechist were probably aspersions due to his obvious jealousy of Akayezu, whose presence undermined for three months the legitimate authority he exerted over the church outpost that the fathers had entrusted to him.

It seems Akayezu did not distinguish himself in the years he spent at the minor seminary in Kabgayi. His professors had nonetheless noted that he was a solitary student of few words, who worried them a little, as a minor semi-narian should never keep apart from the others but rather join with humility and docility in the community of those whom God has elected for the priesthood. Rumours had also reached them about the strange conduct Akayezu sometimes indulged in during his holidays on his hillside. But in his defence, he was by far the best student of Latin. The old father Edgar Clays, his Latin instructor, had taken a liking to him. He had given him free access to his personal library which, his colleagues said, contained works that were of dubious orthodoxy, not to say frankly deviant, for the venerable missionary was a scholar of heretical sects of the Church's early centuries. It was, some claimed, those banned books that had finally tipped Akayezu's already fragile mind over the edge.

After his first year in the major seminary, when the long holiday came, Akayezu had refused to join the parish designated by the Superior where, according to the rules, he was supposed to serve a trial period as auxiliary. He stated that he would only go to the parish that oversaw the outpost church on his hillside: he wanted first to evangelise the hillside where he was born and where his people lived. Isn't that what he'd done every year when he was at the minor seminary? The hillside children were expecting him. No one knows why they gave in to his disobedience. Perhaps the pleas on his behalf by his Latin instructor allowed him to bend the rules for three years running.

The priests of the main mission had looked askance on Akayezu returning to their parish, dressed in his major seminarian's cassock. They were all the warier in that he refused the lodgings they offered him and the chores they had reserved for him. Akayezu took up residence in the family enclosure where, as is proper for an adult son, they had built him a hut covered in sheet metal, befitting the dignity of a quasi-padri. In the evenings, after leading the fold in reciting a dozen rosaries, he listened piously to his mother's marvellous stories that captivated her audience. To conclude the evening, Akayezu took the floor and, in the guise of a small sermon, compared Kibogo rising to Heaven to Yezu's ascension, Maria's Assumption, and the abduction of the prophet Elijah on a pikipiki of thunder and flame.

It was the so-called 'resurrection' of little Angelina that gave Akayezu his reputation as a saint for some, and as insane or demon-possessed for quite a few others. It was probably also the stir this 'miracle' caused that led to his expulsion from the major seminary.

One night, Immaculata came to wake the seminarian.

'Akayezu,' said Immaculata, 'get up quickly, you must come, it's Suzana, she's just given birth but the baby – we think it's a girl – is going to die or maybe is dead already. You must baptise this creature, whatever it is, you who are almost a padri, you must wrest her from the clutches of the devil who will throw her into the great fires of Hell and if she is already half-dead, maybe you can give her back the half of life she's missing.'

Akayezu, without thinking it through, but certain it was his priestly duty to save a soul, threw on his cassock and followed Immaculata. In the large hut, the newborn's mother, stretched out on a bed of herbs, was surrounded by the laments of the matronly midwifes. One of them tendered a small reddish-black creature in a lambskin that might indeed have been a girl but gave no sign of breathing.

'You see,' said Immaculata, 'either she's dead or she still has a final breath of life, so don't waste a minute. You have water here in this gourd and also butter in this pot if you need it.'

The matrons pressed their imposing fleshly mass so closely against the seminarian that he was almost smothered.

'Quick, Akayezu, if she isn't dead, you can save her, and if she is dead, perhaps Maria will take pity and catch her just before she falls into the fire that never burns out.'

Akayezu closed his eyes, seemed to meditate intensely, and finally said:

'Bring me that gourd, first I have to bless this water.'

A woman held out the gourd and Akayezu gave his benediction three times. He asked someone to pour a few drops of water into the hollow of his hand and he sprinkled it onto the baby's forehead:

'*In nomine Patris et Filii et Spiritus Sancti*, I, Akayezu, baptise you, whoever you are, whether you be alive or dead.'

'And so what did you call her? She needs a name, for herself and so that her father and mother and everyone on our hillside can be sure she was baptised.'

'Angelina. I name her Angelina, for if she is dead, she is now an angel, and if she lives, her name will always remind her that she nearly became an angel. Now bring me that pot of butter.'

Akayezu took a little butter on the tip of his index and middle fingers and anointed the baby's forehead, lips, chest, stomach, and feet.

'Now, Angelina,' he said, 'I am certain I have fully baptised you.'

At that moment, the newborn produced a feeble wail, flailed its tiny limbs, then emitted a huge cry, the kind it should have made when first out of the womb.

'She's alive!' cried Immaculata. 'She's alive, Akayezu revived her, Akayezu restored her to life!'

The women fell to their knees before the seminarian and kissed his garment.

'He's revived her, he's revived her!' they shouted. 'Akayezu did that, he can raise the dead!'

'It wasn't I,' Akayezu protested in vain, 'I closed my eyes and I saw Maria, the Blessed Virgin, who caught the little girl just as she was about to fall into the pit of Hell.'

'You see,' the women retorted, 'your baptism is powerful, it forced the Mother of God herself to come to the aid of a child who we all knew was stillborn.'

News of Angelina's 'resurrection' soon spread throughout the hillside. Many scoffed at what those women were claiming, those storytellers, those spinners of lies. But the tale was brought to the mission priests, who summoned the seminarian, interrogated him lengthily, rebuked him soundly, and enjoined him to publicly refute this hogwash peddled by ignorant women or perhaps unwittingly inspired in them by the devil himself. Akayezu denied the story without much conviction, embroiling his forced rebuttals in a detailed account of the Virgin's intervention in extremis at the mouth of Hell – which comforted those who believed the story of Angelina's 'resurrection' and its embellishments, but convinced the church fathers that the seminarian was suffering from dangerous mental delusions that were incompatible with his vocation and threatened to subvert the honour of the priesthood. They therefore informed Akayezu via formal letter that he would not be returning to the major seminary when classes resumed, that he was irrevocably dismissed because of his extravagant conduct and his repeated claims that contradicted Catholic dogma. They spared him an excommunication, deeming that the appropriate treatments, assuming he submitted to them with all due humility, could restore him to the path of reason and faith.

The news broke like an improbable thunderclap in the dust-brown sky of the dry season: Akayezu had been expelled from the seminary. It was Bizimana, the chief catechist, who had relayed the rumour circulating around the mission. He spoke of a letter written and sent by the monsignor himself. The priests had confirmed this information, employing many unctuous euphemisms. Akayezu, they said if pressed, had fallen gravely ill. It was his head. From reading too many books. Books he shouldn't have been reading. Books that were too much for the brain of someone better suited to tend his father's cows. The padri especially cautioned against approaching him. He might have been the incarnation of one of those evil spirits that used to fool Rwandans before they, the missionaries, came to reveal the true God to them. Of course, they had chased away Shatani, the great chief of all the devils, but minor devils were still prowling around and could prey on the weak or on those who, like Akayezu, considered themselves smarter than everyone else. Better to be prudent and keep away from him if he insisted on living on the hillside. In any case, the Administrator and the police had him in their sights.

They also said that he'd been ordered by the Father Superior to give back the white cassock of the major seminarians. The parish priest had come in person to the hillside and up to his father's house to deliver a threatening letter. Akayezu had categorically refused to obey, deeming that he was within his rights since he had learned Latin and knew better than the others how to interpret the Bible.

He had, they said, hidden the robe in the untouchable grove, buried under a sacred tree; and yet, when he wore it, for the sermons he delivered at clandestine gatherings that his partisans held in his honour, it was always miraculously spotless.

Moreover, some claimed it was the white robe that made Akayezu into a rebel. At the major seminary, his fellow students used to joke that he had taken the portrait of Pius XII for his own reflection. Dressed in his white cassock, he proclaimed himself more infallible than the Pope.

Akayezu had had to leave the family enclosure; his father, no doubt reluctantly but owing to the shame, had thrown him out despite the supplications of his mother and five sisters. He lived in a small hut deep in the forbidden wood, and the fear inspired by those old trees shielded him from attempts at banishment. In any case, those who tried were few in number, for many considered him a lunatic, and in Rwanda you don't bother lunatics, who are free to wander and rant amid the sane, subject only to the jeers of children. This was now the status imposed on Akayezu by most of the hillside's inhabitants: the village crackpot.

A small number, meanwhile, displayed an unshakable fidelity to Akayezu and believed him inhabited by a powerful spirit, perhaps even the spirit of Yezu himself. His followers, mostly women, came to consult him discreetly in his shack, listened to his interminable sermons that were increasingly peppered with Latin maxims, and, when the flood of eloquence finally ran dry, asked him for advice or healing. Akayezu dispensed his oracles free of charge, but his consultants in gratitude left him bean stews, corn, bananas, sorghum biscuits, pitchers of beer, and so on. It's as if he were under the protection of the women, as he was called upon by desperate mothers expecting him to renew the 'miracle of Angelina' for their own dying child. If the child survived, this recovery was added to the list of prodigious occurrences that burnished Akayezu's legend among the faithful.

Akayezu was more specifically surrounded by a dozen or so women that he called his devotees. Immaculata or one of the devotees brought him his daily meals. He called his benefactresses his pretty crows. They didn't understand why. It made them laugh. Apart from food, they made sure he was never short of beer, swept clean the threshold of his hut, gathered wood for the fire, washed and mended his precious cassock. In return, Akayezu gratified them with one of his endless homilies of which they didn't understand a blessed word but about which the ex-seminarian made them swear not to utter a sound. Immaculata held the role of 'best-loved disciple' and guardian angel.

It's true that for Akayezu she had sacrificed her social standing and her reputation. Immaculata was an orphan. Her entire family had perished in the great famine of 1943. She had been taken in by the Benebikira nuns, the Daughters of the Virgin. They had put her to work cooking, cleaning house, tending the vegetable garden and the fields. She had learned how to embroider placemats that the sisters sold to the few visiting Europeans. She'd also learned to read and write and had acquired a few rudiments of Catechism. With such baggage, she could easily have found a husband if nature hadn't disgraced her. One of her legs was visibly shorter than the other and this infirmity discouraged her rare suitors, the matrons charitably notifying the latter that with her twisted legs, Immaculata's womb could never support the weight of a baby. The nuns had obtained for her the position of auxiliary catechist for the youngest children on the hillside, but the relations she clearly maintained with Akayezu and the aberrations bordering on heresy with which she adorned her lessons (which the chief catechist never failed to note and report to the missionaries) ultimately got her relieved of her duties. She then found refuge with an old widow who had known her parents and who, moreover, was a follower of Akayezu's: she warmly welcomed this woman who seemed to enjoy the Master's favour.

Immaculata thus benefited from a great prestige among the faithful and gladly acted as interpreter, in her way, for the rantings issuing from Akayezu's mouth. She herself harboured a boundless admiration for him, not only for his colourful eloquence but especially for his theological knowledge, which she deemed at least equal, if not superior, to that of the Pope, whom the padri had certified was incapable of error.

And it was in fact to her, his best-loved disciple, that he revealed the arcana of his secret doctrine, but when she was questioned about it, Immaculata replied that she had not retained all of it and especially that she hadn't understood it all. Akayezu assured her that he had read the entire Bible, several times, and from every angle. Because, according to the padri, the Bible could have several meanings. And only they, they claimed, knew the correct one. According to them, the Bible spoke only of Yezu and of nothing else. But he, Akayezu, wasn't so sure. The idea preyed on his mind: 'Tell me, then, why the padri's book never talks about Black people and why it says nothing about us Rwandans? Did Yezu not know any Blacks? Had he never heard of the Rwandans? Did we not interest him? And if I say, "Joshua is Ruganzu Ndori who conquered Rwanda, his kingdom," and if I say that the mupfumu, the divine Elijah who was spirited away to the heavens by a thunderball, is Kibogo, what would you answer?' But when Akayezu asked these questions, the padri shrugged and laughed, or else they grew angry and threatened to expel him from the seminary, which eventually they did.

By now, Akayezu was certain that it wasn't the story of the Jews the Bible told, nor even of Yezu, but of the Rwandans. The padri had obscured everything to fool the hillside populations, the ones who lived at the centre of the world. They had rushed in to convert them to their lies as fast as possible, for fear that the people would discover the truth and become all-powerful.

During the students' daily walks at the major seminary, Akayezu would habitually veer off from his regulation companion and head alone onto the mountain, taking his peculiar ideas with him. There he would recite for himself alone one of his mother's folk tales (his favourite, after the story of Kibogo), the tale of Princess Nyangoma, who was banished from court by her cruel stepmother, the queen, and sent far away to serve as a scarecrow to keep the birds and monkeys out of the corn fields. Standing in the fields with only the birds and monkeys for companions, Nyangoma sang love ballads from morning till night that attracted birds and gazelles instead of scaring them away. Akayezu put into her mouth the love song he'd read in the Bible: *Nigra sum sed pulchra*, which he translated as: 'I am beautiful, for I am black.' And Akayezu followed the path of the clouds, saying: 'These are messages sent to me by Kibogo, for so Saint Paul, who was small and blacker than a mutwa, has written – but his letter to us Rwandans was stolen by the padri: Kibogo shall return on his cloud.'

Immaculata never tired of questioning the seminarian about the celestial marvels he must at least have glimpsed, she was certain of it, in the course of those mysterious studies or on the mountain above the seminary where he had become the shepherd of his thoughts. Then Akayezu described for her, with all due precision, the angels with wings of fire who, in the glowing red depths of the crater of the volcano Karisimbi, joined in the dances of the Kubandwa spirits.

'How can you know all this?' Immaculata sometimes ventured to ask him.

'Two spirits have taken up residence in my head: one is the spirit of Yezu and the other is of Kibogo. That is where they make peace.'

Mathilda, his eldest sister, and Imelda, the youngest, barely fifteen years old, had joined their brother. They had thrown in their lot with the conventicle of matrons who had witnessed the 'resurrection' of Angelina, with the mother of the 'miracle girl', and with two or three so-called 'loose women' who had gone to seek their fortune in Kigali and come back to the hillside humiliated and universally shunned.

MUKAMWEZI

It was toward the end of the dry season that Akayezu undertook to 'evangelise', in his way, old Mukamwezi, the pagan, the witch, the scourge of the hillside – 'back from who knows where, and more's the pity for us', said the catechist. The people of the hillside despised her and kept her at a distance, but they also feared her. They tried to ignore her, and when little children asked the elders who was that old woman who lived all by herself in a miserable shack, far from all the other houses, hidden in a crag of the last foothills of Mount Runani, they were told: 'She's an old madwoman, don't go near her what-ever you do!' And when greeting a member of her clan, they added in mockery: 'And how's Mama Kibogo?' The clan member would pretend not to hear or understand.

Anyway, everyone maintained they didn't know who this Kibogo was or how Mukamwezi could have been his bride. Yes, some might still say that she'd been in the court of King Musinga and his fearsome mother, Queen Mother Kanjogera, that she'd been some kind of priestess, or rather sorceress, and that she'd celebrated satanic rites. But those were evil thoughts that you'd best atone for in confession, for the devil lurked in hidden corners of memories from the time when your ancestors were heathens.

Still, after dark, the tale of Mukamwezi's return was perfect for night-time storytelling, and Akayezu's mother was not among the least liable to embellish its episodes. And so the woman they thought they'd never see again suddenly reappeared like a ghost from the land of the dead. She had built, with the help of who knows who, a small round hut at the foot of the mountain and started cultivating a rudimentary field on rocky soil where it was pointless to expect even a meagre harvest. The legend of Mukamwezi became part of the storytellers' nocturnal repertoire. In it, she was reunited with Kibogo and his retinue behind the clouds and, dancing on the crest of the mountain, she adorned herself with pearls of rain. And the murmur of the story blended with the dreams of the child Akayezu nestled in his mother's pagne, half dozing in the warmth of the hearth, until they were one and the same.

No one would have dared say so aloud, but many were convinced Mukamwezi had risen to Heaven to join her betrothed, Prince Kibogo, and like him, she had saved Rwanda, or at least the hillside, from the drought that threatened to wipe out the entire population. 'Have you truly heard,' some repeated under cloak of darkness, 'have you listened carefully to what the padri told us, to what's written in their big book that they read at Mass? Yezu rose to Heaven and his mother followed after, so it's just what Kibogo and his Mukamwezi did, except in her case she came back.' And Akayezu, long before he went to school, lent an ear to the dotards' gossip, and their tall tales delighted the child's memory.

The day Akayezu resolved to go 'evangelise' old Mukam-wezi, he had not only put his venerable white cassock back on but had also strung around his neck a large-beaded rosary like the priests wore, and several collars decorated his chest like a clinking pectoral of medallions, crosses, glass pearls, bones, and the teeth of various bush animals.

At the threshold of her enclosure, between the bundles of bamboo that framed the doorway, he called to Mukamwezi:

'Yewe, Mukamwezi, yewe, I am Akayezu, I know you are not unaware who I am. I've come to baptise you: be not afraid, it's the Imana of Rwanda who has sent me to you; be not afraid, my baptism is not the same as the padri's.

Let me in, there's no time to lose, I need to speak with you, our Imana told me: "You must baptise Mukamwezi," I am Akayezu, you know who I am. I'm from your hillside. I've brought holy water, a small gourd of banana beer, isongo, and hydromel.'

He repeated his plea five times but received no reply. He sat down at the entrance to the enclosure, on the bed of herbs he had spread out in lieu of a mat.

'Mukamwezi, show yourself, I know you're in there and that the spirits that possess you will not try to chase me away, I have what I need to make them flee,' he said, rattling his medallions. 'I shall not leave here until you answer. I shall not eat until you let me in. I shall willingly die from hunger if you do not answer. And after I die, my umuzimu, my ghost, shall pursue you relentlessly and you too shall be unable to touch any food. Let me come to you. I am little Akayezu, you saw me being born.'

Not until nightfall did the seminarian receive a reply:

'Akayezu, I know who sent you, it's the abakorwa, the hyenas who brought the curse upon our Rwanda. They are not human. Their evil spirits have taken hold of you, and now you too have an evil heart. And you want to splash their poisoned water on my head: don't you think I know all about their little tricks? I, Mukamwezi, I too have a spirit inside me and it's more powerful, it commands the rain.'

'Mukamwezi, if I baptise you, it will not be like in church, it will be at home, we'll drink isongo, and if you want, hydromel will flow over your hair: it will be the baptism of Akayezu. Your Imana told me: "If we marry our spirits, then we'll have more power to save our Rwanda."'

There was a long silence, then came the reply:

'Your hydromel isn't as good as the mwami's. In the court, I drank the king's hydromel, and I'll let you taste it if you come to me. Come in, you and your Imana, and we'll see if your Imana finds favour with mine.'

Rumour – or legend – has it that Mukamwezi and Akayezu stood face to face, shut up in the hut, for an entire moon. But no one ever knew what they said or what they did.

When she realised Akayezu was gone, Immaculata ran frantically over the paths of the hillside, questioning the other followers of the defrocked seminarian. The women answered that they too were worried, for no one had seen Akayezu in two days: they had noticed when bringing his morning meal that his hut stood empty. It was the children who made a game of mockingly trailing Akayezu who told her: 'Go to the pagan's, we saw him enter her hut. Maybe Mukamwezi ate him, since they say she eats

little children, so maybe she also eats men who wear robes.'
Annoyed, Immaculata chased away the brats, who scattered off laughing. An elder who had heard the whole thing snickered:

'Your unholy Akayezu didn't get everything from Yezu; he probably wanted to ask how he could rise into the sky like Kibogo.'

'You shut up, old man,' Immaculata retorted furiously, 'you don't know what you're talking about, you're just babbling and your tongue will bring you misfortune.'

The old man shook his stick angrily and went off grumbling.

Akayezu's sequestration plunged Immaculata into a distress that, with each passing day, grew into a stabbing anxiety.

Every morning, she went up to the sacred wood in hopes of finding Akayezu in his shack. Alas, it was always empty. Immaculata spent the rest of the day prowling around the witch's hut. She strained her ears, but no sound of voices reached her; she lay in wait for hours on end, watching for the occupants of the hut to enter or exit, hoping that one of them would eventually emerge, if only to relieve themselves in the ditch behind the banana plantation. The door remained stubbornly shut. Who could protect Akayezu, save him from Mukamwezi's maleficence? Should she address her prayers to Yezu or else, since he was in a pagan's home, to the pagan spirits that grabbed hold of initiates during the mysteries of Kubandwa? It was probably too late: he had already fallen under the witch's spells.

She confided in Akayezu's devotees, who shared her anxieties and joined in her prayers. They had to save the seminarian from the witch's influence, come what may. He had clearly misjudged her power, Mukamwezi had been the stronger and had made off with him and his Imana. The women consulted at length about finding an antidote. They finally came to an agreement: there was only one remedy to use, the one they gave their children to wrest them from death: milk.

'But,' said one of the matrons, 'not just any milk! We need the milk of a cow who has just calved for the first time, that first, yellow milk, with its thick, rich foam. That's the milk that restores life.'

'And the milker must be a vigorous, skilful young man,' said Mathilda, Akayezu's sister, 'one who can hold the milk jug firmly between his thighs.'

'I know just the one,' said the second matron. 'My youngest son is famous among all the shepherds. But the milk jug, the icyansi, must be a jug that has never held any other milk. We have to be sure of this, and to be safe, best to have one carved specially, and from the wood of a flame tree, no other.'

'And how will we bring him the milk so he can drink it?' said Thereza, the loose woman from Kigali.

'He doesn't have to drink it: this milk is for his Imana,' said the other matron. 'Did you forget the way we do for spirits while you were in the big city? We dip the leaves of a small branch in the milk, then shake it and the droplets suffice.'

'You're right,' said Immaculata, 'and we'll do everything that's been said. But there's something else you haven't thought about. Among Akayezu's Imana, there are also the Imana of the padri. Have you forgotten his name, Akayezu? Because of his name, I believe his Yezu can also help him. And what do we have of those Imana? We have their medallions. The padri say that they're to protect you from evil spirits, illnesses, all sorts of misfortunes. We have to plunge those medallions in the milk jug, and we'll shake the jug well so that their powers will merge and, in the middle of the night, we'll go sprinkle the door and roof of Mukamwezi's hut, from as close as we can get. After that, we'll bury the medallions all around, and I, Immaculata, will be sure to recite the formula the seminarian taught me for banishing evil spirits: *Vade retro, Shatani*. And you, our mothers' incantation: Amata, Amata, kamarashyano, milk, milk, purify all.'

Several women balked at giving up their medallions:

'My medallion,' said the mother of the 'miracle child' Angelina, 'was given to me by Akayezu himself. When my little girl is sick, I place it on her stomach and it kills the worms eating away at her. How will I cure Angelina without my medallion?'

'If you give your medallion like the others,' said Immaculata, 'Akayezu will heal Mukamwezi's evil spells. And if your little girl becomes sick, he himself will cure her.'

Everyone finally agreed to donate their medallion and they prepared, according to the ritual prescriptions they had settled on, the elixir that was to deliver Akayezu from the nefarious bonds holding him captive.

The exorcism took place one night when the clouds hid the moon. But the next day and the days after that, Immaculata and the women waited in vain for Akayezu to reappear. Mukamwezi's sorcery was clearly more formidable than they'd thought.

Every night, Immaculata and the other devotees lamented loudly, no longer knowing who to implore.

'That witch,' Immaculata said over and over, 'that concubine of the devil has dragged poor Akayezu, who only wished to baptise her and save her soul, to the deepest pits of Hell, to the land of shadows where the spirits of the dead wander lost, the abazimu who burn with an insatiable thirst, tongues hanging out, without even a drop of beer from their families. But why couldn't he defend himself, he who learned so many things for so long, whose inexhaustible flow of words could sway the worst miscreant? Mukamwezi is just an old woman. How could she have lured a man as young, handsome, and intelligent as Akayezu? How could he stand to share a mat with that scrawny heap of bones, or caress those withered dugs flapping off her like seed pods from a flame tree? But she's a witch, and no doubt she can transform herself into a beautiful maiden with taut, firm breasts and tempting round buttocks. Yes, Mukamwezi is one-eyed as death, but she's a witch and when she wants to she knows how to make eyes gentler than a heifer's and speak in the soft, enchanting voice of a young virgin. And then who could resist her languorous gazes? Ah, my sisters, what sorrow, what terrible sorrow, let us weep loud and long, for Mukamwezi has taken possession of our Akayezu and never will she give him back and nevermore will we see him!'

The heartrending wails of Akayezu's followers kept the entire hillside awake. But the next morning, everyone swore they hadn't heard a thing.

At sunrise, Immaculata and two other women reached the top of the hillside and entered the forbidden grove, in the middle of which stood Akayezu's hut. They had developed the habit every morning of depositing a small, long-necked gourd filled with sorghum beer, as they would for the spirits of the deceased. They ritually swept the floor and threshold of the hut, freshened the herbs in the absent one's mat, and burned a few fragrant leaves in a smudge dish. At the door of the hut, they embraced each other lengthily, exchanged laments on Akayezu's disappearance, and heaped the most terrible curses on his presumed kidnapper who, they said, had dragged him to the deepest pit of Hell.

But that morning, at the very back of the hut, they thought they could make out a white shape in the shadow of the thatched vault. They were already falling over one another in terror to flee the umuzimu, who was clearly the spirit of poor Akayezu brought to death by the torments of Mukamwezi, when they heard the voice of the ghost calling them back:

'Why are you afraid? Don't you recognise me? It's me, it's only me, I'm here, it's me, Akayezu, here before you alive and well!'

They turned around and saw Akayezu, standing tall in his immaculate robe, his hand raised in blessing.

'Is it really you, Akayezu?' they cried. 'You're really alive! You've escaped the witch! You conquered her!'

'It's really me. Come here so that I might touch you, feel my hands, which are not the hands of a ghost.'

They sat around Akayezu.

'Yes,' they said, 'we recognise the power of your hands: you really are Akayezu.'

'In three nights, it will be a full moon. Come back here, all three of you, under these trees inhabited by spirits.

I shall reveal great secrets to you and I will not be alone. You must prepare a large pitcher of sorghum beer and a small one of hydromel that you will leave in my hut the day before. Tell no one I'm here and on the night when you come to join me take great care not to be followed. Go now, with my blessing on you and your Imana.'

One by one they emerged from the hut, and Immaculata, glancing back a final time, thought she saw the white silhouette wavering in the perfumed smoke that rose from the dish.

The devotees waited impatiently for the night of the third day. Akayezu had apparently disappeared again. Immaculata wondered anxiously whether Mukamwezi had again ensnared him in her magic net. She no longer knew where to address her prayers: she had appealed to everyone and everything. The women prepared the large pitcher of banana beer and a smaller one of honeyed sorghum beer as Akayezu had asked, and discreetly deposited them in his hut in the sacred woods. They took turns standing guard near Mukamwezi's shanty in the hope and especially the dread of seeing Akayezu there, but they detected no human presence.

The clearing in the grove where stood Akayezu's hut was lit by the pallid light of the moon. The seminarian's disciples noticed immediately that their pitchers were arrayed around the furrowed, blackened trunk of a large ficus that had been struck by lightning. Akayezu emerged from his hut and invited them to sit in a circle around the pitchers, beneath the shredded branches of the tree. His white cassock seemed to reflect the lunar brightness, and on his chest hung a dozen rosaries adorned with animal claws and sachets made of bark cloth.

Akayezu tendered them a straw and, at his invitation, each of the women took a sip of beer from the large pitcher and of hydromel from the smaller one.

'Blessed are you to have come this far,' Akayezu said, 'especially if you retain what you are about to hear.'

Akayezu pushed aside the large pitcher and the disciples saw in the tree's split trunk what seemed to be an old woman squatting, wrapped in a dark blue pagne.

'Mukamwezi!' cried Immaculata. 'Why have you brought that poisoner here among us?'

'Akayezu,' the devout moaned in chorus, 'you have deceived us, you want the old witch to grab hold of us the way she's done with you, quick, we have to get away!'

'Stay where you are,' said Akayezu, 'and listen to me.'

The women huddled together, trembling. The supposed Mukamwezi had covered her face with a flap of her pagne.

'What are you afraid of?' continued Akayezu. 'Mukamwezi and I have joined our Imana, by a blood pact we have united them. It's the Imana of Mukamwezi who is speaking to you with my voice. Listen to what her spirit has to say:

"Our Rwanda no longer has a king, no longer has a mwami. The one pretending to be, who has usurped the regnal name Mutara, is not the mwami of Rwanda, but the mwami of the Whites. When they banished his father, did he not accept the drum from their hands? And did our sages enthrone him according to ritual? He preferred to drink with them the hydromel they call champagne! And the hill on which his father's palace stood he gave to the padri; and where we should venerate the untouchable trees, they built their church. And it was Mutara himself who proclaimed that Yezu was now the king of Rwanda; and our sacred drums, which are the roots of Rwanda, were dragged like captives before the statue of their Yezu. And so we need a new mwami for our Rwanda, and all will be as it was before."'

Mukamwezi stood up. She suddenly appeared very tall to the women sitting at her feet. They noticed that her face was not withered and the brightness of her eyes made them lower their gaze.

'I, Mukamwezi, you know who I am: I am she who was dedicated to the spirit of Kibogo. It was the duty of my lineage to give a virgin to worship the Imana of Kibogo who saved Rwanda, it was the honour of our clan. I, Mukamwezi, have remained faithful to Kibogo, I am *his* bride, not Akayezu's. I have known no man; the spirit of

Kibogo visits me, in my dreams or through signs. Akayezu listened to the tales told by his mother. Now it's Kibogo himself he hears through my mouth. It's as if he were my son. Hear me, then, all of you: the padri preach that their Yezu rose to Heaven and because he rose to Heaven, he shall return. They say that the sky will then turn red, that the lightning will spare no one, the mountains will crumble, deafening trumpets will sound in the clouds as with the soldiers on the Belgians' holiday. The padri say all this, but I said to Akayezu: Who will you believe? What the padri say, or what your mother relates in the evening after dark? And you women, who should you believe: what they taught you in Catechism or what the spirit of Kibogo has revealed to me? For this I tell you: Kibogo has risen to Heaven, and he shall return. He has risen to Heaven from our mountain, and he shall return on our mountain. And where the lightning struck him to carry him beyond the clouds, there the lightning shall set him down. All the thunder's drums shall acclaim Kibogo and Kibogo shall proclaim, "I am your mwami, the one who has come to save Rwanda," and all the drums shall rumble without being beaten and all the people shall clap their hands together: "Ganza umwami! Ganza Kibogo! Long rule the king! Long rule Kibogo!" But in order for this to happen, and it's the spirit of Kibogo who revealed it to me, Akayezu must be taken away to Heaven. He must go in search of Kibogo, and thus, like Kibogo, he shall be a saviour, an umutabazi, for our Rwanda. It is Akayezu whom Kibogo has chosen as guide when he descends from Heaven; it is Akayezu who shall clear a path for him through the clouds, who shall summon the storms, who shall walk before him on our hillside. All this I have seen in a dream.'

The more Mukamwezi spoke, the tighter the women huddled together. Only Immaculata dared ask a question:

'And when shall Akayezu be lifted into Heaven? And when shall Kibogo return?'

'When the rains return, and they shall return soon. I know this, they are near. When the storm breaks out, a storm such as no one has ever seen on the hillside and to which we'll give a name, we shall climb Mount Runani and at the forbidden place, on the horn of the mountain, there where the lighting took Kibogo: there you, Akayezu, shall stand, and I, Mukamwezi, shall brandish the Inkuba spear, the Thunder-Spear, and if the lightning wishes and Kibogo wills it, we shall enter the clouds and the lightning will bring us to Kibogo. Then Kibogo shall descend on the clouds and we shall be carried to meet him and I shall say to him: "Kibogo, hear us, we have come before you; I am your bride, I have remained faithful to you, and Akayezu here is ready to take his place before the clouds to show you the way, and you, Kibogo, shall return to save Rwanda, you shall be our new mwami, you shall drive out the padri and all the Bazungu." And during this time, you women shall remain at the foot of the mountain and wait there to acclaim the mwami who has come down from the stormy sky, for a king must be welcomed into his Rwanda by the cheering of women.'

Immaculata's gaze, fixed on Akayezu, had become ecstatic, but the others turned away, and Thereza, who had led a dissolute life in Kigali and Bujumbura and to the hillside's great shame had brought back with her two mestizo children, murmured loudly enough to be heard:

'This is all just politics. I don't want any part of it. If the sub-chief learns what you have in mind, he'll send his police, and if it's the Belgian, he'll bring in Congolese soldiers from Kigali and we'll go to prison and the entire hillside will get fined or worse.'

She was standing up to leave, but Mukamwezi held her with the power of her stare and forced her to sit back down.

'It is useless to run away,' said Mukamwezi, 'you have followed Akayezu, you will accompany him to the end, until Kibogo comes. You can no longer escape. What you have drunk from the pitchers was not banana beer, was not hydromel, but igihango, the Secret of Kibogo; it is what should have been drunk by those idiots to whom the secrets of Rwanda were revealed, for if they betrayed the secrets of Rwanda, the igihango would turn into poison, and you, if you betray the secret of Kibogo, you will fall dead on the spot. You have no choice: acclaim Kibogo as the new mwami or you shall all die.'

The women cried out in terror but Immaculata shouted:

'Ganza Kibogo! Ganza umwami! Long rule Kibogo! Long rule the mwami!'

Trembling, the women repeated the acclamations, but much more quietly.

When it was noticed that Akayezu had moved into Mukamwezi's round hut at the foot of the mountain, the people exclaimed:

'And now our crazy seminarian has taken the old witch for a wife, it was surely the devil who married them, or the spirits! This can't mean anything good for our hillside!'

They kept an eye out for the women who visited them daily, bringing them pitchers of beer and stews of beans and bananas:

'Have you got a load of his concubines?' they said. 'They have no shame: Immaculata with the gimpy leg who renounced Yezu, and that ninny who believes Akayezu revived her daughter, and those loose women who brought back from Kigali all sorts of maladies along with their bastards, and now the apostate is prostituting his sisters, even Ismelda, the youngest, who isn't even fifteen!'

The catechist was of a mind to denounce this scandal to the padri or the sub-chief, but most felt that it could only bring trouble to the hillside. They'd accuse everyone of being in league with the witches. Safer to act as if they hadn't seen anything.

The children started a wicked rumour that disturbed the evening gatherings and the talk around pitchers of beer. They claimed that while following Immaculata, as was their wont, and taunting her about being a nutty cripple and the devil's concubine, they'd heard her mutter:

'Bunch of ignoramuses, if you only knew what I know. But you will never find out until He comes, and He will come with the rains.'

As some saw it, the marriage between she who had been betrothed to the spirit of Kibogo and he who had stolen the wisdom of the padri and been driven insane could only augur the greatest ill.

The impatience with which they typically waited for the first rains was now mixed with vague apprehension.

The rainy season started that year with a storm so violent that the women and even the men, stricken with fear, implored the protection of Yezu, Maria, Ryangombe, Kibogo, and all the spirits, good or evil. Some jangled rosaries, others gourd rattles, or the bones of warthogs or of their ancestors. Children wailed in their mothers' arms, who tried to pacify them by singing ancient lullabies between their own sobs. Clouds enveloped Mount Runani, turning it into a grumbling mountain of shadows and flames. For three days running, thunder, lightning, hail, and torrential rains beat down on the hillside. Rivers of mud flowed down the mountain paths, washing away several huts along with their inhabitants, while others, smashed to pieces by the squalls, ended up without a roof or walls.

When the storm moved off to devastate other hillsides, they saw that Mukamwezi's shack had been flattened under an avalanche of boulders and that the lightning that had struck the old trees in the sacred wood had set fire to Akayezu's hut, of which only a small pile of ash remained. It was assumed that both of them had perished, either under the heap of rocks or in the flames, but no trace was found of their corpses.

As they had done so many times after many other misfortunes, they rebuilt the clay walls and went to beg for sheet metal from the subchief and the mission. The sub-chief promised to compile a report for the Administrator and confided this delicate mission to his clerk; the latter grumbled that he already had a ton of paperwork to draw up, but that a case of beer just might help him find the time. The padri gave a few sacks of beans and two cans of powdered milk for the babies. They pointed out with satisfaction that the brick building of the church outpost had not suffered any damage, proof positive that it had been protected by Yezu and Maria and that everyone should thank them. The pagans who still clung to their abominations, for their part, had been hit hard. The padri added that someday they would have to erect a statue of Maria at the top of the mountain to remind the inhabitants of the hillside and their descendants of the graces she had bestowed and would continue to bestow if they prayed to her with sincere hearts.

Akayezu's followers dispersed and tried to stay out of sight. They said that Immaculata had thrown herself at the padri's feet to beg their forgiveness. She remained kneeling a long time at the door of the main mission church, where the missionaries refused her entry. The one in charge of the church outpost on our hillside finally agreed to hear her confession and, after public repentances, they took her on (perhaps to keep a closer eye on her) to work in the mission chicken yard and pigsty. There were those who claimed that she still accused herself in the privacy of the confessional of succumbing to the temptation to look up toward the top of Mount Runani, but surely this was pure slander, for what sacrilegious ear would dare eavesdrop on what a sinner told her confessor!

The loose women and their bastards went back to Kigali where they again hoped to market their wilted charms. Soon nothing more was heard of them.

The missionaries persuaded the Benebikira nuns, the Daughters of the Virgin, to take Akayezu's sisters Mathilda and Imelda, who dared not return to their father's house, into the convent to save their poor young souls led astray by their cursed brother. At the convent, they learned how to cook and sew as civilised people do. They were mistreated by the novices, who never lost an opportunity to strike these she-devils, in order, they said, to expel the demon that still possessed them. They were placed as servant girls in the families of Belgian volunteers, but they also say that Imelda ended up marrying a young American Adventist pastor, to the outrage of the entire convent.

Angelina, the 'miracle girl', was rebaptised following the orthodox rites, but her mother was finally allowed to let her daughter keep the name Akayezu had given her. When the little girl reached the age of five, rumour spread that, thanks to that dual baptism, and especially thanks to the one Akayezu had administered, the child had inherited miraculous gifts and that, if she touched her playmates, their booboos would immediately heal. Soon people were coming to consult the diminutive healer for children who had suffered a bad fall or injured themselves trying to manipulate a hoe that was too big for them. From this, Angelina's mother derived a certain profit.

Whether it was Yezu's umuzimu still angry with the pagans or the ancestral spirits offended at seeing their cult abandoned, everyone agreed that only a very powerful spirit could have unleashed such a storm. No one knew at present what to do. They even regretted that Akayezu had vanished, for he knew so many things and no doubt would have offered good advice, even in his madness.

Sometime after the great storm, some kids started telling a bizarre story to anyone who'd listen. There were three of them, Kabwa, Gatwa, and Gahene, the hillside trouble-makers, always ready to pull a practical joke to aggravate the dignified matrons, or make up stories to frighten gullible little girls, or spread malicious gossip that got neighbours into fights. There was no one to discipline them. Their fathers had gone off to the mines in Katanga and were no longer heard from, evidently held captive by the Congolese women's spells. Our three hooligans lorded it over their abandoned mothers, brothers, and sisters like little masters of their enclosures. They had made the lower slopes of Mount Runani their favourite hangout. No one dared chase them out because of the interdiction that weighed on the mountain. There they hid their loot and peacefully enjoyed the fruits of their petty thefts: ears of corn, peanuts, sweet sugar cane stalks, bananas . . . and even those multicoloured candies lifted from the Swahili's shop or extorted from the daughters of the 'advanced', in other words, the medical orderly and the agronomist.

Still, despite their witless recklessness, they hadn't yet dared venture to the top of the mountain, not quite sure whether to give credence to the legends that claimed Kibogo had been abducted into the clouds and that those imprudent enough to climb up would be struck by lightning or, in the dry season, carried off by a whirlwind.

After much hesitation and debate, the little hoodlums decided that, being too old to believe in their mothers' fairy tales and the gibberings of oldsters who only spoke in proverbs, they'd go see for themselves what was hiding up there.

'Maybe,' said Gahene, 'the Whites from before the Belgians left their treasure there when they fled, maybe they buried sacks of roupias, coins with their king and his feathered helmet on them, I've seen some, the Belgians pay a fortune for them.'

'No,' said Kabwa, 'it must be the bones of a former mwami buried there, maybe even Kibogo's bones. The Bazungu dig to find the skulls and bones of the dead. I don't know what they do with them, maybe eat them? If we show them where to find a bone, they'd give us a good reward.'

'Or else,' suggested Gatwa, 'from what I hear there's a beast up there, a monkey three times bigger than a man like on the Muhabura volcano. And the Whites like monkeys, if we showed them an animal like that, imagine what cash we'd get, what amafranga!'

The story that the three good-for-nothings hastened to tell when they returned all atremble from their excursion made the rounds of the enclosures in just a few evenings, no doubt gathering numerous embellishments along the way.

So, they had set out to scale the mountain under a perfectly clear sky but, at some distance from the crest, they were suddenly enveloped by a thick cloud. Gahene and Gatwa said: 'We'd better head back, we can't see a thing, we could fall off a cliff, and besides you know what they say about Kibogo and his cloud, and don't you guys think this cloud looks kind of weird?' But Kabwa insisted: 'You're scared of a cloud! You believe in all those old wives' tales about Kibogo! We're not kids any more. We can't turn back so close to the top. You're just scaredy-cats!' They kept on climbing, one behind the other, a hand resting on the shoulder of the one in front so as not to get lost. Kabwa went first. The cottony waves of fog seemed intent on swallowing them whole, taking on strange, fleeting shapes that disintegrated in impalpable specks as soon as the boys approached.

Reaching what seemed to be the summit, they thought they saw a shape that, instead of dissolving into the mist, appeared to gain in consistency and assume a quasi-human form the closer they came. Kabwa swore he'd seen a very old, very skinny woman wrapped in a tattered pagne but with eyes burning red like the embers on which you grill corn. The two others protested, saying the apparition had nothing human about it and that they had seen, when they spread their fingers (for they had covered their faces with their hands so as not to be blinded by the demon) a skeleton with shreds of desiccated flesh hanging from it. In the end, all of them agreed that they'd been dealing with an umuzimu, a ghost, rather than a living creature.

The supposed phantom had moved toward them and they were about to hightail it when the voice of the umuzimu held them fast like a hunter's net:

'Where do you think you're going, you little rascals? What have you come here for? Don't you know this place is forbidden? Who knows what misfortunes you'll call down upon yourselves, and on the entire hillside?'

'We're just children,' said Kabwa, 'how could we have known?'

'Shut your mouth, you little liar. I know who you are, all three of you ... And you, do you know who I am? I believe you've all recognised me.'

'I think,' said Gahene, 'I think you might be Mukamwezi, or rather her umuzimu.'

'I am whatever you wish, but listen well, all three of you, and tell this to everyone on the hillside, without leaving out or adding anything. When the great storm came, Akayezu and I climbed Mount Runani to the top, in this very spot where you are. We came in search of Kibogo who had saved Rwanda. We hoped he was inside the cloud, that he had returned to save Rwanda anew. Then, Akayezu and I entered into the great cloud that had buried the mountain. I cannot describe how many bolts of lightning lit the inside of the cloud and how the thunder echoed louder than a thousand drums. The lightning blinded me and the thunder made me deaf. And yet, with my blind eyes, I saw the lightning set Akayezu ablaze like a torch of dry grass and, with my blind eyes, yes, I tell you, I saw him rise into the sky, carried off in a whirlwind of fire. And so I know that Akayezu has gone beyond the clouds to join Kibogo and that he'll bring him back, on the clouds, to save our Rwanda again and again. Say this to everyone on the hillside, tell them this story, this story will be your talisman, it will protect you from the curse you should have suffered for coming here. It's here that I, Mukamwezi, wish to wait for death, it is right nearby, I can see it with my blind eyes, and it has Kibogo's face. And now run, run, flee down the slope as fast as your legs will carry you for fear that it doesn't catch you as well, for death is insatiable.'

When the urchins told their tale, everyone told them to hush, that these weren't things to repeat to every passer-by, that they should just forget all about it. The catechist threatened to denounce them to the padri; their story had clearly been inspired by Satan, prince of liars, for it was neither Kibogo nor Akayezu who was meant to return on a cloud, but Yezu himself. There were no other stories worth telling.

And yet the tale of Akayezu, though forbidden, was taken up by several of the storytellers. They wove it into the legend of Kibogo and spun a yarn that they reserved for evening's end, for the few women who had managed to stave off sleep, while the men dozed around the empty pitcher. And sometimes, a little girl, forgotten at the story-teller's feet, who refused to go to sleep like the others, stored away in her memory, without really understanding them, the enchanted words of the fable.

KIBOGO

Bazungu like the ones who came during the dry season –
that was something they'd never seen before.

And yet, all sorts of Bazungu had passed through the
hillside! First there were the padri, who seemed to have
been there forever. There was the one who came to the
church outpost now and then to lead a Mass and take
confession from anyone with a sin to admit, and then the
ones from the main mission; it was finally decided they
weren't entirely white, so accustomed was everyone to
those old greybeards, and their weird way of pronouncing
Kinyarwanda no longer made people laugh: they were just
padri. And then there had been other padri, young ones
freshly arrived, who spoke among themselves a language
that wasn't like the old padri's, and who remained Bazungu

as far as everyone was concerned. They said they'd come to Rwanda specifically to help the poor, the lambs of God, and that *their* Yezu didn't like people who owned large herds of cattle and kept them for themselves, and the chiefs who made the poor populace work without paying them – they hated those people. The old padri, in their schools, had created troupes of intore dancers; the new ones created soccer teams. The dancers were bare-chested and had sisal manes like the warriors of old; the soccer players had shorts and undershirts like the Bazungu children.

And then there were the Bazungu who wanted to teach the peasants how to farm, the agronomists. They said they would show how to garden like them, because those poor peasants didn't even know, as they did, how to plant in tight, straight lines, and that was how you had to plant. That it was bad to mix everything up, let the bean shoots climb up the corn stalks and, worse still, under the banana trees! You had to keep all that separate: each crop in its plot. And besides, they said, there were too many bananas, the banana plantation had to be 'thinned out'. And the poor peasants cut down their banana trees, including, with rage in their hearts, the intuntu whose bananas are used to make beer. And above all, they had to plant coffee trees. The coffee trees took up all their time and almost all the room, while their daily bread, the beans and sweet potatoes, were neglected. Everything that had been saved to fertilise the soil – the corn and sorghum stems, the dried banana leaves – now went toward mulching the coffee trees. Woe unto the neglectful, on whom fines rained down, not to mention twenty lashes with the chicotte. But the agronomist wasn't the meanest one: it was the Rwandan agricultural supervisor who followed his master around like a little dog. He was proud, scornful. How could he make these ignorant peasants understand what the agronomist was saying? The supervisor wore boots and the peasants went barefoot.

There were also the Bazungu who rode by in cars. No one knew how they'd strayed onto our path. It was an event people talked about for a long time: 'Did you see the Bazungu go by?' Even rarer were the ones who stopped and got out of the car to photograph a small girl with her earthen jar on her head. Terrified, the girl ran away, her jar shattering on the ground, and lost the scrap of cloth that barely covered her little behind. The young boys came running, shouting: 'Muzungu! Muzungu!' The Whites quickly got back in the car and sped off. The little girl's father boasted: 'The Bazungu tried to steal my daughter, but when they saw me coming with my stick, they took off without claiming their due.'

One day, a few came to photograph the old trees. They took measurements. They jotted everything down in their notebooks. They asked the catechist, who spoke a little French, what he knew about that grove farther up the hill. The catechist said that it dated from the time of the pagans, that no one went there any more. The Bazungu seemed satisfied with what the catechist had said: they carried it all away in their notebooks. The catechist said he thought he understood that they were going to build a clinic there. These days there are no more trees, only a statue of the Virgin.

It was the sub-chief who came to announce the arrival of these new Bazungu:

'Whites will come,' he said, 'great bwanas, especially one who has come especially from Europe just to see you, just for your hillside. He's a scientist, you have to call him Professor, you understand, not Boss, just Professor. He wants to see your elders, he wants them to tell him stories from the olden days, from very long ago, from before Musinga, before the Belgians, from the time of Ruganzu Ndori, of Gihanga, of Adam and Eve, who knows! You do have elders here, don't you? Old ones who still know those imigani, those tales, those cock-and-bull stories you drag out at night. The Professor wants all that stuff. And he'll be here next week. Take me to me your elders, I want to see them now, I want to know if they're still able to get two words out.'

There weren't many oldsters left on the hillside. Most had died, first because they were old, and also from tuberculosis, and malaria, and all the other old-person illnesses. There were still Karekezi and Gasana, but those two really were too old. Anything they had to say no one could understand: they stuttered, they stammered, they got everything jumbled up and repeated themselves a hundred times over. No one paid any attention to their babbling, except for the children because they thought it was funny and they repeated the two old men's ditties for laughs. And besides, they were still half-pagan. Did the Whites want to listen to pagans?

'That's right,' the sub-chief had said, 'perfect, that's exactly what I need. Old people who keep repeating the same old stories and who are half-pagan: that's what the new Bazungu want, they came especially for that. And for something else too, they say there's something hidden under the hill where the statue of Maria is, I didn't fully understand what they told me in Astrida, a queen's tomb, a watering place that cows came out of, I don't know, and they also believe that at the top of your Mount Runani, some strange things happened involving someone named Kibogo. You ever heard of him?'

Naturally they had all heard of Kibogo, even if the story was best forgotten. But what seemed even more worrisome was that the Bazungu had heard of Kibogo. Whoever could have told them about that? They'd never be through with this Kibogo business! But it might have been the fault of that little hoodlum Kabwa, who had managed to get accepted to high school, goodness knows how, while his buddies Gahene and Gatwa had remained in the village. Kabwa told everyone, especially the Whites, that where he came from, on a mountain called Runani, he had seen the ghost of a witch, and there were also skeletons and heaps of bones, he couldn't say if they were animal or human bones, that his grandmother told strange stories about that mountain, involving a certain Kibogo who had risen into the sky from there, or maybe others had come from the clouds to look for him. A young Belgian teacher had taken an interest in his story. Where I come from, he explained, they tell the same things: on the moon, in the stars, there were certainly living beings that they called extraterrestrials and those inhabitants of the sky came, especially in more recent times, to visit Earth and even abduct humans. According to him, this was certainly what had happened to Kibogo. Our ne'er-do-well offered to guide his teacher to the top of Mount Runani if he bought him shoes. The volunteer teacher wanted to spend the night on the mountain to observe the heavens. Kabwa wrapped himself in the blanket his teacher had brought and went to sleep. When he awoke, the teacher claimed he had been up all night and seen many strange lights. Kabwa lost no time in spreading the story and embroidering it: he told his awestruck friends that in the night sky they had seen a huge brightly lit machine that someday soon would bring Kibogo back to Earth. The tale reached the ears of the Father Principal, who immediately summoned the professor and sharply reprimanded him for corrupting a naïve population with his crazy ideas, especially young people on whom the nascent Church of Rwanda grounded its most fervent hopes. He therefore found himself obliged not to renew his contract for the next semester and ordered him to stop spreading that gobbledygook about extraterrestrials to anybody, especially his pupils. Kabwa was expelled from school and went back with his two old friends to prowling the hillside looking for trouble.

The sub-chief had insisted on seeing the two old men who'd been recommended to him. He wanted to make them understand that professors had come from Europe just to see them and especially to hear the old folktales from distant times that only they still knew.

'What do those Bazungu want from me?' said Karekezi. 'Do they know me? Do I know them? And why should I have to know them? And my stories, even if I still know them, don't interest anyone around here any more, so why would they interest the Bazungu? If it's just to poke fun at a poor old man like me, as the rest of you do, I have nothing to say to them.'

Karekezi concluded his tirade with a jet of saliva browned by his tobacco wad.

'The Bazungu did not cross the oceans and travel all the way to your hillside to make fun of you. They want to write down the stories you remember, they want to take them away i Burayi, to Europe, so they can put them in their book.'

'They're going to write down what I tell them? In a book, a book like the Bible?'

'That's right, Granddad, whatever you tell them they'll put in their book, and it will even have your name, Karekezi. Can you read your name?'

'I can read and write my name! No more than that, but it's enough. What do you take me for, a savage? But look at me, do you see how I'm dressed? Worse than a savage! My trousers have holes, they're holding together by a thread, and it's my only pair. My shirt has lost all its colour and its buttons. What will the Bazungu think when they see me like this? They're going to say, "Rwandans abandon their elders and let them die in poverty." Shame upon our country!'

'Granddad, we'll buy you a nice shirt and a nice white pagne so that you can do us honour with the professors.'

'Trousers, I'd rather have trousers.'

'No, the visitors want you in a pagne. Aren't you an elder? You have to dress like an elder. But if you speak well, like the professors want, afterward we'll buy you trousers for your great-grandchildren's weddings.'

'And will I also have an agacupa, a little banknote? If the professors want nice stories, they'll have to give me amafranga. The Whites are rich and these ones must be very rich if they've come from so far away just to hear a poor old man.'

'You'll have your money: when the Whites really want something, they're prepared to pay a lot for it, and what they want are your stories.'

The sub-chief then went to Gasana and made the same promises.

'I've forgotten all that,' said Gasana, 'but I'll tell them everything. And I'll have my name in the Bazungu's book too.'

The new Bazungu arrived one week later in a huge Land Rover. There were four of them, accompanied by two young Rwandans. The district commissioner who had served as their guide hurried to open the door for the important bwana. The local councillor had advised everyone always to call him Professor. It was a bit disappointing that this great Professor was not wearing trousers but rather a pair of khaki shorts, like schoolboys' kabutura but longer, much longer, down to his knees, and white socks that stretched to the top of his calves without quite managing to reach the shorts. Everyone hated the professor's fat knees. On the other hand, they admired his jacket because of its countless pockets. His narrow-brimmed hat didn't raise any eyebrows: the agronomist, the one who boasted to his supervisors that he'd slaughtered entire herds of elephants and buffalo, had the same kind, a safari hat. Finally, they noticed that his beard was much shorter than the missionaries', though no one knew if that meant anything. His companions hopped from the back of the car: two young men and a young woman, dressed more or less like their boss. There was much commentary about the fact that the girl wore trousers, the outfit of a sinebwana, a woman-with-no-man. But they took pride in the fact that the two Rwandans, in suits and ties as if for a wedding, had safeguarded the national dignity.

The professor, having greeted with polite warmth the delegation assigned to welcome them, asked via one of the Rwandans whether it might be possible to go visit the elders prior to the oral investigation of which they were to be the subjects: he wanted to start straight away forming a trusting relationship with them, which was necessary in order for him, through an interview that would be informal but conducted with all due scientific rigour, to mine and preserve the historical riches that their memories still contained. And he added in sententious tones: 'Even peoples without writing have their libraries.' The professor's retinue vigorously nodded at his words. One of the young Rwandans hastened to jot them down in his notebook.

The commissioner, who seemed ill at ease, added that the district was planning to open a library. It was only waiting for the books. The hillside councillor went over to say something in his ear. The commissioner cleared his throat several times, then finally addressed the professor:

'Mister Eminent Professor, Sir, permit me to suggest to you that, perhaps, if I may say so, or in fact it seems to me, it would be better, it might be wiser to postpone your visit to our elders until tomorrow, just until tomorrow. They have not been notified of your visit, they haven't had a chance to prepare for it, to see someone as important as yourself enter their simple hut, it could be a shock to them, they are just feeble old men, the entire population watches over them, they have to be treated gently. We're going to explain the whole thing to them, so that they fully understand what it is you wish of them, that it's for the honour of our country that they may speak to you, we'll plan all of that, find a suitable spot where they can tell you their stories, and where you can listen to them in complete tranquillity.'

'Fine,' said the professor, 'we'll start the interviews tomorrow. But please tell your elders that we have come with all good intentions and for the good of Rwanda. A new country such as yours can only base its foundation on a scientific knowledge of its past. So as not to waste the day, perhaps we can go up to the sacred wood to give it a first once-over.'

One of the Rwandan guides (we eventually understood that these were students from the university in Astrida, taught by the three Europeans who, themselves, seemed to be disciples of the professor) conveyed the request to the hillside councillor. The latter seemed embarrassed:

'The Kigabiro? Well, that is, there is no more Kigabiro, the trees were all cut down, they died, they were very old . . .'

'What do you mean, cut down?'

'They'll explain it to you . . .' said the commissioner, 'but, Mister Professor, Sir, it's getting late, I believe it's time to head back to reach the Agronomic Institute before nightfall, and for me to be driven back to the commune.'

'Very well,' said the professor, visibly irritated, 'we'll see about all this tomorrow.'

Everyone wondered why the Bazungu were being housed at the Agronomic Institute, which was farther from the hillside than the mission church, where the occasional travellers usually stayed. No doubt about it, these new Bazungu did nothing the usual way.

The evening and much of the night was spent preparing the two old men. Despite their vigorous protests, they finally agreed to let their great-granddaughters wash and dress them. Beneath the pitchers of water that the little girls emptied over them, they shook, trembling and moaning like the spirits of the dead that haunt the marsh. Gasana demanded, since they were treating him like a young bride before her wedding, a few drops from the bottle of amarachi, the perfume that one of his daughters-in-law, as he well knew, bought at the Pakistani's behind her husband's back. Karekezi hurled curses against everyone on and around the hillside and swore that those Bazungu monsters would not get a single word out of him. Their leathery old bodies were dried with tufts of herbs, ishinge, and they were wrapped in the kind of grey blankets that the zamu in Kigali have, who guard the villas of the rich. They split with the notables a pitcher of banana beer. Each one had the privilege of savouring for himself alone a bottle of Primus that the commissioner had left for them. Which put them in a jovial mood: they began telling stories and singing. 'No, not yet,' they were told, 'save that for the professors. Now go to sleep on your mat.'

At sunrise, the two elders were woken and, decked out in their splendid shirts and handsome new, dazzling white pagnes, were installed in folding chairs that had been set up under the thatched overhang of the cabaret where the hillside notables gathered every evening around a pitcher of banana beer. Following the students' directions, they had borrowed a table from the councillor. Gasana refused the chair and demanded a mat on which he squatted, leaning on his shepherd's staff. Everyone had long to wait, as the professors' car didn't arrive until mid-morning. The professor greeted the two old men respectfully, warmly thanked the councillor and all those who had assisted in preparing the interview, but asked them to remove the curious onlookers who had gathered around the cabaret. The councillor and the catechist had some difficulty persuading the crowd to disperse. A few blows with the rod finally dissuaded the most recalcitrant. During this time, the students had unfolded canvas chairs and arranged on the table the equipment that would gather and preserve the old ones' words. They accepted an offer of help from three young boys, one of whom seemed to know a little French, advising them to be very careful: 'You have no idea how expensive a Nagra is! And fragile!' The three boys were granted the privilege of staying for the interview session, if they kept quiet.

The students scrupulously took down the name, lineage, and genealogy of the two oldsters. Karekezi listed nine ancestors and Gasana eleven. Karekezi claimed that he was born before the arrival of the Digidigi, the Germans, when Mwami Rwabugiri was warring with the Bashi who are now in the Congo; Gasana, in the time of the great plague that had killed off almost all the cows and announced the arrival of the Bazungu. The professor and his three assistants asked questions, which the students translated.

The professor began by stating that he'd come from Europe expressly to listen to them because he'd heard about this hillside. He knew its story. He had read about it in books. The story was that of Kibogo. He wanted to hear it from the mouths of those who surely knew it better than anyone else because they lived at the foot of Mount Runani. He wanted to discover with their help whether the story of Kibogo might conceal others.

Karekezi told how, to save Rwanda from famine, a famine like the one that had raged during the last war that the Bazungu waged among themselves, one of the king's sons, named Kibogo, had been chosen by the soothsayers to be sacrificed and save the country that was on the verge of perishing. And this Kibogo was also called Akayezu. He wore a beautiful white habit like the padri and he spoke the language of the padri, like in Mass when they speak to their Imana. And so, as they were about to sacrifice Kibogo, who was also this Akayezu, at the top of Mount Runani, up there, on that mountain right over there, just above us, a cloud came to fetch him and he rose up to Heaven like the padri's Yezu and perhaps someday he too will return.

'All this,' Karekezi went on, 'I didn't witness myself, I heard about it from the old ones of my time. But Akayezu, when the great storm came, went up the mountain and we never saw him again. And I heard that he had with him an old sorceress who claimed to be his bride but was more like the Maria of Yezu. They also say that like him she went up to Heaven, I don't know how, but others have claimed they saw her ghost on the mountain and I don't know who might have said such things, but they're surely just tall tales.'

'No, no, no,' Gasana interrupted, 'don't listen to him, Karekezi doesn't know what he's talking about. He's old. He gets everything mixed up. It wasn't during the war among the Whites that Kibogo went up to Heaven. It was long before they came here. It was . . . who can remember? In the time of Mwami Ruzanzu or maybe another, who knows, but what I do know is that it wasn't a cloud that abducted Kibogo: it was lightning that struck him, and not just him but also his five wives and twenty children and his intore who surpassed all the others in dance as well as in combat and his beef cattle, his inyambo, that no one could count because he owned so many: the lightning struck all of them, and so then they could all enter the great cloud that carried them off into the sky. Yes, that's how Kibogo rose to Heaven. This I heard from my father, who got it from his father, who got it from his father . . . And this is why it's forbidden for anyone to climb Mount Runani, for one must not tread upon the spot where lightning struck, and those who have tried have never returned. May I myself be struck by lightning if I'm not speaking the truth!'

Karekezi protested:

'Don't listen to Gasana, he's a liar, and he's senile, he's too old. Everything he just said is false. Everybody here knows he just makes up stories for anyone who has the patience to listen.'

'Calm down,' the students replied, 'I'm sure the professor will like what Gasana said and what you said as well. We'll try to translate for him what you've just told us.'

The professor seemed a bit disappointed by what the old men had recounted. He pressed the students to keep asking questions:

'But I also read that at the mwami's court, there was a hut, an ingoro, a sanctuary dedicated to Kibogo. Tell me about this. Do you know how Kibogo was worshipped? And there was also that young girl, that virgin, the vestal who'd been betrothed to him ...'

'It's true,' answered Karekezi, 'there was a girl from these parts who was sent to the royal court to look after Kibogo's hut. She was like a servant, she swept out the enclosure. But the girl's family is no longer here, they left, and she disappeared, no one knows what became of her.'

'But,' one student persisted, 'the professor would like to know exactly how Kibogo's umuzimu was worshipped.'

'It's a secret. No one can know. Only those who hold the secrets of Rwanda, the abiru, have this knowledge. I can tell you nothing about this. Have you seen where the sun is? I don't want to change into a lizard.'

'But the professor was told that there were people, back then, who had been killed on the mountain, that's what he'd like to know about.'

Gasana, who was nodding while listening to Karekezi, then spoke up:

'Karekezi says he knows nothing about this. That's true, but I do know. And I, Gasana, will answer your questions.

And you will tell your professor that I'm the one who spoke the best, so I'm the one he must give compensation, amafranga menshi, money, a lot of it.'

'He'll give you some if you speak well, as he wants. Try to remember: apart from Kibogo, were there others who died up there on your mountain to make the rains come? Try your best to remember, perhaps they killed people there.'

'Well, then, I'll tell you … Kibogo's bride, for the young girl was the bride of Kibogo, Nyirakibogo, was responsible for the rain since Kibogo had brought the rains onto Rwanda. But if the rains were late in coming, if the rain refused to irrigate the Rwandans' fields, the rainmakers said to the mwami, "The rain wants a sacrifice, Kibogo is calling for his bride." So then they brought out Nyirakibogo, they made her climb Mount Runani and they threw her from the mountaintop or arranged it, don't ask me how, so the lightning would strike her, which was even better for making the rain come …'

'Don't listen to him,' whined Karekezi, 'he's talking nonsense, how can he make up such things, for our shame and that of all Rwanda? He's greedy, he'll do anything for amafranga, and even for a little sip from the agacupa. If you don't make him shut his big mouth, he'll just keep piling on more and more. What shame for our hillside! What great misfortune for our Rwanda!'

'Why did they bring her up Mount Runani for her sacrifice?' asked the professor, increasingly interested.

Gasana reflected a long while before answering.

'It's just that ... I have to remember ... I didn't see this with my own eyes ... It was the old people when I was a little child who told what they had heard from their grandparents and that they themselves ... All right, so why did they throw Nyirakibogo from the top of Mount Runani? It's because there's an overhanging rock for that purpose. It juts out over the abyss. And so they pushed her to the end of it and she fell all the way down, onto the rocks, and she was smashed against the sharp boulders. And they left her for the vultures and hyenas to devour, and that's when the rain decided to fall. You can go up and see the overhang, it's still there.'

'Yes,' said the professor, 'I understand: they sent her to join Kibogo. She was his bride, they sacrificed her on the same spot as he, on the mountain. But you haven't really told me, does the Kigabiro have anything to do with this?'

'The Kigabiro? Yes, the Kigabiro, indeed, the Kigabiro, I almost forgot ... It's coming back to me now ... The Kigabiro was the domain of Nyirakibogo. She went there to ask for rain, the mwami sent her, that's where she had her cows and her intore ... maybe sometimes they also sacrificed a cow and an intore, I'm not sure any more ... Will that do, is the professor happy? That's enough, I spoke well, no?'

'Yes, that's fine, don't add too much more or you'll get it all mixed up. I'll translate everything you've said for him.

I think he'll be very happy, as he's been searching all over for human sacrifices, it's his specialty!'

'Good,' the professor said after hearing out the student, 'interesting, interesting. Tomorrow we'll go explore the Kigabiro, or at least what's left of it. It's a shame they cut down those ancient trees, those witnesses to Rwandan history. Wasn't there anyone to protect them from the missionaries' vandalism, to save such a precious patrimony!'

No one understood why these new Bazungu were so interested in the trees on the hillside when all that remained of them were stumps. Why they asked so many questions about them. It was as if they were angry over those old trees, that it was a sin to have cut them down. The catechist tried to explain, and one of the Rwandan students translated his plea.

'Those trees,' he had argued, 'dated from the time of the pagans. It was the devil and his possessed who had planted them. They held ceremonies there that no one will want to tell you about now that everyone has been baptised. Do not ask these questions. Everyone has forgotten all that, all those pagan charades. Besides, God's fury had fallen on those cursed trees. During the great storm, many were struck down. They dried out and fell to dust. The people of the hillside had nothing to do with it.'

What the catechist related was for the new Bazungu's benefit, but it wasn't entirely the truth. In fact, the people of the hillside had helped God's fury along a bit. Or more precisely, they had helped the Xaveri to, as they said, 'topple the idols'. The Xaveri came from the main mission school. A new principal had been appointed: one of those new padri who talked only about progress and demokarasi. He had enrolled some of the students in a movement they called the Xaveri. The old padri's intore danced, the Xaveri played soccer. The intore had to be tall, slim, and supple; the Xaveri soccer players squat and stocky. A major seminarian who'd been put in charge of forming the squad of Xaveri for his trial stage had selected his players and told them:

'You footballers are the true Rwandans. The intore are little girls dressed up as ancient warriors. Their ancestors are from Ethiopia or, worse, Egypt.'

The principal, for his part, spoke to his troops about their holy Patron, Saint Francis Xavier, the great missionary who had gone to the ends of the earth to baptise the Japanese. Nagasaki, Yokohama: these names appealed to the Xaveri: they were like Rwandan names. The Xaveri had received handsome uniforms, shorts with khaki shirts. Almost like the army. And like the army, they had banners, yellow and white, the pope's colours, standards showing the Blessed Virgin on golden clouds. The girls from the home economics school had embroidered Maria and the clouds. The Xaveri sang songs that had never been heard at Mass. The padri accompanied them on his accordion.

> Boldly to the summits,
> We Xaveri have followed
> The steep path of progress
> And development.
> The sun shines on Nyanza
> Ever since our king
> Gave our country to the King of Kings.

The principal was very fond of a game called theatre. He explained that it was a game in which you have to pretend to be someone else and declaim the other person's words as if they were your own. The Xaveri had played the martyrs of Uganda. The martyrs were like intore that the wicked king of that country had thrown onto a large pyre because they refused to renounce Christ and yield to the tyrant's abominable customs. The performance had taken place on 30 June, the day of the Feast of the Martyrs of Uganda, and it had been much discussed at the cabaret among the more sophisticated members of the chiefdom.

Personally, the principal seemed sorry that King Musinga, a hardened pagan, had not, like the Ugandan king, inflicted martyrdom on some of his intore who had received baptism. Rwanda had botched its entry into the Christian religion.

The principal was so proud of his initial success that he told the Xaveri they would soon rehearse and quickly perform another play. It had been written long ago by a Frenchman named after a bird, but of course he had translated it into Kinyarwanda with all the appropriate adaptations. It took place in the time of the Romans who had conquered the entire world with the sole exception of Rwanda. The Romans were pagans and they perse-cuted the Christians. The play told the story of a young soldier who, having just been baptised, immediately tried to smash the idols. He was executed on the spot by the soldiers guarding the idol.

The performance was held one Sunday after High Mass, reserved for the students and the elite. The idol looked like a scarecrow, only more horrible. They had hung the most disgusting grisgris from it. The padri himself had drawn the grimacing features, with an open mouth full of ferocious teeth. The newly baptised soldier had rushed up to the false god and smitten it with a single blow of his spear. The idol had collapsed with a deafening noise while the Roman soldiers sporting helmets of gold-painted cardboard belaboured the courageous Christian with wooden machetes. The martyr's white tunic then became stained bright red while a voice, mysteriously dropping from the sky, proclaimed: 'The blood of martyrs is the seed of Christians.' Many spectators had been impressed, but some had muttered, 'All in all, the movies in Kigali are better,' and the Xaveri complained that an intore had been chosen to play the holy martyr and not a footballer.

The Xaveri would have liked to smash some idols of their own (even without the threat of martyrdom), but there were no more idols in Rwanda because everyone had been baptised. The captain of the soccer team suggested that maybe they could go shatter the Karinga drum, for that royal drum was indeed a kind of idol. Under Musinga, the king who had been deposed for intractable paganism, they still daubed it with the blood of sacrificed bulls, as one did for heathen fetishes. 'And maybe even human blood,' insinuated the centre forward. 'Besides, you know what it's decorated with? Bikondo! And you know what bikondo are? Well, pardon me for being vulgar, but bikondo are testicles, yes, that's right, the balls of vanquished kings, and I'll tell you something else: among those vanquished kings, there were Rwandans like us!' The centre forward was shaking with rage and his companions, growing worried, did their best to calm him. If the king preserved Karinga, some said, it's because it's the emblem of the country, a little like the Belgians' flag. If you destroy Karinga, you risk destroying the country. And besides, others added, in Nyanza, the mwami's palace is well guarded, and they won't let you through with your hoe or your machete. The goalie found the right argument to appease the captain's fury: 'I was in Nyanza,' he said, 'when Mutara Rudahigwa dedicated Rwanda to Christ the King. They held a grand procession. Karinga and its suite of drums were in the parade. I can't say they looked all that proud behind the crosses and banners, and the monstrance shining like a sun. Karinga and its suite of old drums – there were eight, I counted them – looked like prisoners. They reminded me of the chained kings that the Romans, like the Father Principal told us, made march behind the victorious general as a humiliation. I tell you, that day, Karinga and the others submitted to God and the padri. Those rotting antiques aren't worth destroying!'

The Father Principal found a way to satisfy his Xaveri's fever to go smash idols. No one knows who might have told him that, not far from the mission, there was a hillside and a pagan grove at the foot of a mountain that people thought was haunted by a demon, or whispered to him that there remained in that lost pocket a handful of hypocrites who went at night to traffic with the devil, a lair of witches and poisoners. And besides, they had added, not so long ago some mighty funny things had gone on involving a defrocked seminarian who had led a gaggle of madwomen into perdition, along with an even more horrifying sorceress who terrorised the poor peasants with evil spells that she'd learned as the high priestess who conjured up the devil. The populace, still blinded by superstitions, had refused to cut down those cursed trees and erect in their place a statue of the bountiful Virgin who would ward off the calamities that still afflicted them.

The Father Principal, having lent credence to these calumnies, had chosen that hill for the Xaveri's holiday camp. Not only would the Xaveri help the poor peasants improve their lot, but they would combat paganism in what was surely one of its last strongholds.

At the beginning of the dry season, a caravan arrived on the hillside the likes of which no one had ever seen. The Father Principal's car led two trucks, one carrying the Xaveri, throats and flags at full throttle, the other stuffed with their camping equipment. The community councillor had come to welcome them. On the day of communal labour, he had them clear an area on the slope of the hill at the top of which stood several old pruned ficus trees, vestiges of the pagan grove. The councillor welcomed the arrivals, thanking the Father Principal for having brought to this out-of-the-way hillside these advanced Christian youths who would sensitise the peasant masses to progress and development. The Father Principal answered briefly that the Xaveri had come to aid the entire population, without distinction, but also to combat the last obstacles of superstition that still impeded – but not for long – Rwanda's entry into the congress of civilised nations.

For two weeks, the Xaveri crisscrossed the hillside, asking from one enclosure to the next how they might be of service. The inhabitants were suspicious and answered that everything was fine and they didn't need anybody and they'd never asked for anything but that if such learned young persons would kindly accept to share a pitcher of beer with humble peasants such as themselves, they would always be welcome and the peasants would be honoured. The Xaveri finally managed to convince an old woman to let them buttress her shaky hut with some new thatching and to prop up her fence, but when the Father Principal asked them to go fetch the crone some water, they flatly refused, saying the chore was unworthy of a man, even a baptised one, and all the men on the hillside agreed. One team paved the way to the church outpost with gravel and replaced the roof tiles the winds had carried off. Another team hacked through the path leading up to the little grove that people said was still haunted by spirits. They couldn't understand why these young folk were putting so much energy into clearing a path no one would ever use.

Every evening, in their encampment, the Xaveri sat around a huge campfire and sang songs, then the Father Principal said a few words to them and, after prayers, they went to their tents. The Father Principal had turned the outpost chapel into his own bedroom and study. The young men apparently paid no mind to the loose women who suddenly materialised and roamed around the tents. But certain rumours, mean-spirited as always, claimed that one of them gave birth in Kigali nine months after the Xaveri's camp.

After the Sunday high mass, the Father Principal spoke. He thanked all the inhabitants for the warm welcome they'd shown the Xaveri and underscored that they had come expressly to help the people. Then suddenly, after a long pause, he stretched out his arm toward the hillside opposite the one on which the outpost stood: 'Turn around,' he bellowed, 'and look well: what do you see at the top of that hill? I'll tell you what I see: a grove that is still pagan. And you live in the shadow of the devil, since those demonic trees are still there and you have not had enough faith to cut them down. Therefore you have not eradicated from your souls, baptised though they might be, the roots of superstition. My Xaveri came to you to free you from all the bonds in which the old paganism still holds you, and that has brought so much ruin down upon you. Tomorrow you will come back here with your machetes and I will bless them and we shall climb the hillside where the demon has taken refuge. To the strongest among you I shall lend these axes, and beneath their blows those trees of the devil will fall.'

The following day, led by the Father Principal and Xaveri brandishing axes and banners, some twenty men, trailed by as many curious women and children, climbed the hill to the pagan wood. The sacred grove was fairly sparse. Many of its old trees had been struck by lightning. Their cracked, blackened trunks jutted from the ground, along with leafless branches reduced to stubs, like giants that were wounded but still baleful. Some thought that their roots stretched all the way down to the land of the dead, where spirits ceaselessly wandered in darkness without end. The improvised lumberjacks from the hillside, like the Xaveri, hesitated a long while. A few women quietly slipped away, then ran down the hill as fast as their legs could go. The Father Principal grabbed an axe and attacked the thickest tree. The Xaveri, suddenly liberated from the fear that had paralysed them, pounced on the other trees. A few hillside men followed the catechist with greater or lesser enthusiasm. The Xaveri put so much fervour and persistence into the task that by morning's end the grove was flattened. They stacked the trunks and branches into a huge pyre that took three days to burn. Five Xaveri watched over the blaze, chasing away the little girls come to gather kindling for the family hearth. 'Don't you know this wood is cursed,' they said, 'the roots of these trees fed on the flames of Hell. Do you want to warm your mother's home with fire from Shatani's kitchen?' The little girls ran down the hill in tears, saying they'd seen the fires of Hell.

The Father Principal congratulated the Xaveri on having exorcised and purified, thanks to their courage, the last of the devil's dens.

The Xaveri, who had planted their banners in the deforested hilltop, carried up bricks and built what they said was a base, as in the main mission church, on which they would set a statue of the Virgin. She was very white, with eyes blue like her veil. The Father Principal explained that the monsignor of Kabgayi had sent a statue of the Virgin to all the large missions but that, as an exception, because the Xaveri had enjoyed the best welcome right here, and because everyone had helped chase away the demons, he had managed to convince the monsignor to reserve one for this tiny outpost. This was a great honour. The inhabitants should be proud and come as often as possible to pray to the good Maria who from now on would protect them and keep them safe from the forces of evil. They recited a number of rosaries, then the Xaveri folded their tents, the Father Principal got into his car, the Xaveri into their covered truck, and the convoy disappeared in a cloud of dust.

The next day, the councillor, the catechist, and several notables welcomed the professor and his retinue at the foot of the Kigabiro hill.

'Don't anyone follow them,' the councillor had ordered the small waiting crowd.

But the three boys rushed to the Land Rover and offered to help the students carry their equipment.

'Fine,' said one, 'but what are your names?'

'I'm Kabwa, and this is Gatwa and Gahene.'

'Your names aren't very pretty,' the students laughed.

'Well, then, call us whatever you like,' answered Kabwa, 'Tintin, Tarzan, Lucky Luke . . .'

'Well, how about that!' the students marvelled. 'Where did you learn about those things?'

'I went to school,' said Kabwa. 'I was even friendly with one of the teachers. He gave me comic books to read.'

'And you're not in school any more?'

'I had some problems with the principal, because of that same teacher. He saw things in the sky, things he called flying saucers.'

The students burst out laughing and said:

'Fine, all right, you can carry the equipment, but don't do anything foolish, and don't go getting underfoot.'

At the top of Kigabiro, the professor, his assistants, and the two students engaged in various activities. They counted the stumps of the felled trees one by one, photographed a few trunks, measured the perimeter of the former sacred grove. From these vestiges, the young woman assistant drew up the presumed map of the enclosure. They gave the three boys shovels and hoes to clear a rectangle of terrain around the statue. The professor lengthily examined the uncovered soil. The students sifted the dirt. They found a few shards of pottery and charred twigs. The professor declared that these were evidently traces of a collapsed hut, perhaps the sanctuary of Kibogo and his priestess. He would recommend that the Institute in Astrida send a team of archaeologists without delay. For that, they would have to move the statue: 'It's as if,' the professor remarked, 'they erected it here to forbid the Rwandans from reclaiming their past.' He was hoping that below it they would find graves, drums, weapons for sacrifices. From the trunks, they could tell how old the trees were . . . All this would be written up in a paper that would be a landmark in African Studies.

The catechist ventured a remark:

'But Maria, her statue, you can't touch that, it was the monsignor himself who gave it to our hillside, we can't touch it, it would be a sin, a mortal sin, and it would surely bring us great misfortune. No, no, you cannot . . .'

'Come now,' said the professor, 'we're just going to move your statue over a bit: the Blessed Virgin isn't going to stand in the way of science, is she? It's like being in the Vendée, or Brittany,' the professor added for his assistants' benefit.

The three boys had quietly approached the students:

'You're sure the professor is going to give us something, right?'

'Yes, of course, he promised.'

'If he gives us a good matabiche, we too could tell a story; we know things, too. Not like that fibber Gasana who says whatever comes into his head for a bottle of beer. Kibogo's wife never had a hut here on Kigabiro and people were never thrown off the mountaintop. Gasana made all that up so he'd get more amafranga than Karekezi. But we can tell you what we saw with our own eyes.'

'Tell us first, and we'll see if it's interesting.'

'If we tell you, you'll go repeat it to the professor and we won't get anything.'

'If it's worthwhile, I'll take you to the professor myself and you can tell him.'

'All right, so you know what we found at the foot of the statue, the wood ash and bits of pottery: none of that's old. We were little then, but we saw it. In the place of the Maria, there was Akayezu's shack. Do you know about Akayezu? He was once a seminarian, and he went crazy. That's why they kicked him out of the major seminary. We're not sure if he thought he was Yezu because of his name, or Kibogo because of the legends his mother used to tell. There were a ton of stories they used to tell about him. Like my grandmother's tales. He gave bread to all the children: with just two loaves, he had enough for everybody. They said he'd revived a baby, now she's a little girl who's a healer. He had apostles like Yezu, but his apostles were women, even loose women who'd come back from Kigali with their half-breeds and their diseases. And then he got married to Mukamwezi. You don't know Mukamwezi? Well, that's going to interest the professor! Mukamwezi was the girl they chose to go to the mwami's court. Mukamwezi was the last one to go to Nyanza. And do you know what she did in the court of the old mwami Musinga? She tended Kibogo's hut. She was Kibogo's girlfriend. Kibogo had this kind of chapel at the king's court. You must know that, since you're practically scholars already, and you also know Kibogo rose into the sky to go find the rain. You've heard the old men's stories. Well, when the great drought came, the one they called Ruzagayura, during the last war, Mukamwezi went up the mountain with the old men, the same two who told you their stories, the others are dead now, and she's the one who made the rains come back. That's what they say behind the padri's backs.'

'Yes, all right, the professor might be interested in your story . . .'

'Wait, there's more. So, as we were saying, crazy Akayezu moved in with Mukamwezi. I don't know who was crazier. One year, at the start of the rainy season, there was a storm like we'd never seen. It destroyed everything, swept it all away. The trees of Kigabiro were felled by lightning. Akayezu's hut burned down. Mukamwezi's shack was crushed by boulders. Everyone said, "Those heathens are dead, they were punished by the God of the padri." But we happen to know they didn't die like that. If they're even dead! We went to take a look at the top of Runani. We went there because it's forbidden by custom. We wanted to know what was being hidden. So the three of us climbed up there, Gahene, Gatwa, and I – Kabwa – and when we'd almost reached the top, we got caught in this strange cloud. We couldn't see a thing. And yet, in that strange cloud, we made out something, I can't say what it was, but that something spoke to us, it might have been an umuzimu, a ghost, the ghost of Mukamwezi, yes, Mukamwezi, but I can't say any more than that, it would bring us misfortune. Unless . . .'

'Go on, I'm sure your story will interest the professor. He'll give you whatever you ask, as long as it's reasonable.'

'All right, well, then,' said Kabwa, lowering his voice, 'the ghost said that Akayezu had gone up into the cloud, like Kibogo, and that he'd return like Yezu.'

'What a story! Where did you get that from? You, Kabwa, come tell your story to the professor. He'll arrange to put it in his book for the other professors. But don't talk too much about Yezu. The professor doesn't really care for Jesus and missionaries. On the other hand, he loves human sacrifices: he goes looking for them everywhere, in his region, in what used to be called Gaul in the time of his ancestors and among the ancient Americans and all over the world. So don't tell him Gasana made up his stories, he'll be very unhappy. But if we can offer him the kind of stories he likes, we hope he'll find us a grant to go to a university in Europe. And don't worry, you'll get a good reward. It's important he comes back from his trip to Rwanda satisfied.'

It was Kabwa who immediately seized the microphone and told the professor, in French, the story of Akayezu and Mukamwezi. Gahene and Gatwa tried their best to introduce a few variants, but the students not so gently pushed them back and made them keep quiet.

'Interesting, very interesting,' the professor concluded. 'Dagobert and Léonidas, transcribe what he told me immediately, so that I can think about it overnight, and tomorrow we'll scale that famous forbidden mountain. These kids can be our guides. Dorothée, don't forget to help them out as they deserve. But I don't want anybody else, and especially not that catechist with his religious claptrap. We don't have any time to waste, so keep him away from me.'

The three boys of course showed up at the appointed hour at the foothills of Mount Runani. They didn't have long to wait. The professor's Land Rover soon came to join them. They gave Gahene and Gatwa the equipment to haul, but Kabwa, promoted to guide, was exempted from having to carry anything and set off in front. He led the little column, making out the traces of a barely perceptible path that grew steeper and steeper as they climbed.

'Not so fast,' the students said, 'the professor is elderly. He has a weak heart. Old white professors are like infants, you have to take special care of them. If you keep up this pace, he'll get out of breath and won't be able to make it to the top. And it will be your fault, in which case you can kiss your matabiche goodbye.'

Kabwa slowed down and they took as many breaks as the professor needed.

'Believe me,' the latter said, 'I've gone up quite a few of these, including the three hundred and sixty-five steps of the great Maya pyramid in Mexico in one go: that was something else! From up top, they used to hurl the bodies of sacrificial victims. Perhaps they also did that from the top of this mountain, according to what the old men and Kabwa told me. In any case, it remains to be seen.'

'You'll surely prove it if such was the case,' the assistants replied in chorus.

'Maybe that's how Mukamwezi threw Akayezu from the top of the rock face. Unless he leapt off it himself. Akayezu thought he was Kibogo. He wanted to rise into the sky, he was crazy,' said Kabwa.

'Or else it was the other way around,' the professor answered with a laugh, 'and it was Akayezu who threw Mukamwezi off. To each his own theory, my boy.'

'He's very smart, this boy,' the professor assessed, 'we should do something with him. You're called Kabwa, that means "little dog". I think your father should have made that "clever little dog". Meantime, do you mind if I lean on you? You're going to be the crutch of my old age till we reach the top.'

The small troupe, Kabwa at the head, helped, supported, and hoisted the professor in the steepest passages, until they reached the sloping plateau that formed the crest of Mount Runani and ended in a rocky spur hanging over the void.

The professor had caught his breath and regained his enthusiasm:

'You see that boulder over there? It's just what I said, Rwanda's answer to the Tarpeian Rock, the great pyramid of Central Africa. It's the sacrificial rock. Make sure to photograph this site from every angle.'

The assistants pulled cameras from their shoulder bags and snapped away at the crest, while the professor seemed to be immersed in deep reflections.

'Now I'll need someone who isn't afraid of heights. We have to go to the end of the spur to see if there might be any signs carved into the stone; I'm not expecting an actual inscription, of course, we're in Rwanda, not the Yucatan. But even so, it's worth checking.'

Everyone hesitated. The assistants kept their faces in their notes. The students pretended not to hear.

'I'll go,' said Kabwa. 'I'm not afraid. I'll let you know if I see anything.'

Gahene and Gatwa tried to hold their friend back:

'You're crazy, Kabwa. Don't go. You're not going to get yourself killed for a Muzungu.'

'Leave me alone,' said Kabwa, 'I know what I'm doing, I'm not an old woman.'

And already he had started onto the narrow promontory, advancing step by step, using his arms to keep his balance. Sometimes he appeared to falter.

'Kabwa!' his two friends cried, 'Come back, you're going to fall, we don't want you to die! What will we tell your poor mother?'

The professor, his assistants, and the two students stared at the tightrope walker, petrified.

Kabwa had reached the far end of the suspended rock. He managed to kneel, and lengthily studied the extremity of the spur.

'I don't see anything,' he shouted back, 'but it's possible they carved this stone a bit. It's pretty pointed.'

On the way back, Kabwa seemed to take large strides, as if he had overcome vertigo or the call of the void.

The professor enthusiastically greeted the intrepid explorer:

'Well done, boy! You're not afraid of anything, on top of which you've got ideas in your head. It is indeed possible they worked the stone a bit. If you stare at it closely, you'll see it looks like the beak of a bird of prey. That's where you take off from. Did you get pictures of that?'

'Yes, definitely, Professor. It's true, if you look closely, it's amazing, it's just like an eagle's beak.'

'Isn't it? All right, now we have to rake off this whole

summit. Maybe we'll find other clues. Don't let anything get by you.'

Everyone examined the parcel of ground that the female assistant had assigned them. Gahene, Gatwa, and Kabwa gathered a few pebbles that seemed oddly shaped. But the professor decided that these were just the work of nature. The assistants came back empty-handed. Then one of the students suddenly cried out:

'Come look! Here are some bones, surely human bones!'

Everyone ran up. Against a rock, you could indeed make out the remains of a skeleton, clearly human, but whose bones had been crushed, mangled, and scattered, as if every predator on the mountain, hyenas, jackals, and vultures, had fought over the carcass.

'Don't touch a thing,' said the professor, 'take photos first.'

'It's Mukamwezi,' murmured Kabwa, 'the misfortune is upon us! We saw her umuzimu, and now, her bones. Her ghost will take its revenge, it will torment us until the day we die.'

'Yes, yes,' Gahene insisted to the students, 'don't touch it. Leave her there where she wanted to die. Her umuzimu must remain on the mountain or it will spread misfortune everywhere.'

'Come, come,' said the professor, 'let's not be supersti-tious. We'll carefully gather up all these remains to study who they might have belonged to. Maybe to Kibogo's priestess, as Kabwa seems to believe, or perhaps the defrocked seminarian, as I suspect. But who knows? They might even be older than that.'

The students let the professor's assistants collect the skeleton fragments. The three boys stayed back a good distance and turned their faces away when they exhumed what might have been a piece of skull.

'It's like the remains of a cannibal feast,' the assistants joked.

Everyone else pretended not to hear. They also found a warthog's tusk, wildcat fangs, glass pearls that must have belonged to a necklace, and even a medallion of the Blessed Virgin.

'Let's hurry up,' one of the students suddenly said, 'look at that cloud, it's running alongside the crest, uncoiling like a snake, it's coming toward us, we're going to get caught in the fog!'

'Yes,' the boys begged, 'we have to go back down quickly before the cloud swallows us up. It's Bweramvura, the cloud of the first rain, Kibogo's rain, he's the one who's sent it to us. We're going to be carried off or struck by lightning.'

Gatwa and Gahene, followed closely by the two Rwandan students, immediately fled down the mountain, leaving the professor and his adjuncts behind. Only Kabwa remained at the professor's side and acted as his guide in the increasingly dense fog that seemed to chase after them. He propped up the professor when he stumbled on the slippery rocks, supported him in the steepest passages, held him back from toppling over the edge. The assistants groped their way behind. They finally managed to reach the Land Rover, in the shelter of which the students and the two boys were waiting. They hastened to make room for the new arrivals, who gave them neither a word nor a glance. The Land Rover started up. The professor, regaining his breath and his spirits, endeavoured to break the glacial silence:

'Well, that was a narrow escape,' he said. 'We were being pursued by the curse of Kibogo, but my friend Kabwa saved me just as we were about to be carried off by the cloud. Maybe Kibogo didn't want me, for what could an old man do in the clouds?'

The students forced a laugh.

'In any case,' the professor continued, 'I will never forget what this young man did for us. Isn't that right, Dorothée? We'll have to take care of him.'

'Of course, Professor,' replied the young assistant, 'but what would the young man like?'

'To go back to school, but this time a real school, a school for Whites.'

'We'll take care of that. We'll surely find a grant somewhere. But tell me, you've got an awfully funny name. Don't you have another name, Kabwa the little dog?'

'It's the name my father gave me. I don't have any other name.'

'Why did he call you that?'

'My father was prudent. And distrustful. In my family, many of my older brothers and sisters had died. I'm his only son. There was no way of knowing whether this malediction came from the Rwandan Imana or the padri's God. So he gave me the name Kabwa to protect me. Why should one of our Imana, not to mention the all-powerful God of the priests, pay any attention to a little dog? We hoped he'd have better things to do. And by the way, it's the same for my friends: Gahene means little goat, and the worst is Gatwa, little pygmy – I'd rather be a little dog!'

'Your father was a sage, Kabwa, a true philosopher. But if you go back to school, as I hope, I'll find you another name.'

'As you wish, Professor, but then you too will be my father.'

'We'll see, we'll see . . .'

The professor wanted to go say hello to the hillside councillor. He wasn't hard to find: nightfall was the time for Primus, so he could only be at the cabaret with the catechist and a few notables. The councillor greeted the professor and his retinue with relief and curiosity:

'So Kibogo didn't carry you off in his cloud! We got worried when we heard the storm rumbling up there on the mountain.'

'As you see, my dear Councillor, Kibogo didn't want us, we're too white.'

'And did you make any interesting discoveries?'

'Yes, I think so. We'll talk more tomorrow. I would like to tell you, Councillor, as well as any of your citizens who are interested, about what we believe we've discovered and what our plans are. For we are not done with your hillside.'

'You will always be welcome, Mister Professor, Sir, and the population will always be at your service. But,' he added, casting a look of disdain and anger at the three boys, 'we will make sure, with your permission, to furnish you with honourable and competent personnel.'

'I believe I've already found what I need,' the professor replied.

Few people the next day came to hear the professor. The catechist had gone from enclosure to enclosure, saying:

'Don't subject yourselves to the fancy words of that crazy scientist. He's a liar. The missionary priests told me: "The Communists sent him to stir up the Lord's humble lambs." Don't you know that he is one of those who worship the devil, Shatani himself, the ones who sacrifice newborn infants on their altars? Isn't that what this professor has come to do on our hillside? He said he'd come back to topple our statue of Maria and put in her place a horrible fetish of the devil, and on the mountain, he believes we used to sacrifice human beings to the idols, he's looking for bones of the dead for his evil spells, for as the padri told me, he's even worse than a Communist, he's a Freemason! And for the Whites, Freemasons are like pagan for us, going off at night to make Kubandwa with all the demons of the brush: they speak to the dead, they dance with the devil!'

Everyone barricaded the entrance to their enclosure with interlaced thorn branches, those who had padlocks padlocked their huts, the men kept their machetes near at hand, and the women strapped their newborns tight against their backs.

Nonetheless, the councillor managed to persuade a few of his citizens by promising that the professor would surely offer a round of Primus before his departure to thank the hillside for its hospitality. Of the two old men, only Karekezi deigned to go greet the one he now called his Patron and Benefactor; Gasana refused, complaining that although he had said the most to make the professors happy, he'd received the same amount as Karekezi, who had said nothing.

The professor's pompous speech was approximatively translated by the students. He maintained that his research would revolutionise the history of Rwanda and Central Africa, to the dismay of his colleagues timidly shut inside their universities. He himself was a man of the field. He would soon be back and was going to train onsite competent youths like the ones he had met here, he concluded, looking at Kabwa. The councillor asked if the honoured

Professor could help them convince the authorities in Kigali to build them a community clinic. The professor answered that the discoveries he would surely reveal on the site of the former sacred wood and on Mount Runani would make the hillside famous the world over. He even had plans to reconstruct the sanctuary of Kibogo and his vestal. To attract enlightened tourists, they could re-enact the rituals once celebrated there. He was certain that this would have enormous success and bring much revenue to the village. They would need drums, intore dancers, and they would select a very pretty young girl to play the role of Kibogo's predestined bride. He was counting on the cooperation of all the inhabitants and he was certain this would incite the authorities to provide the hillside with the necessary infrastructure. The students discreetly reminded the professor that the custom was not to leave without having a drink to 'seal their friendship' and the councillor therefore invited all who wished to honour the professor to follow him to the cabaret where they had set out the requisite Primus and banana beer. A small crowd was already waiting under the straw roofs, despite the catechist's directives. Soon the beer was flowing freely and the number of those who desired to wish the eminent professor bon voyage had visibly swelled. Kabwa tried his best to protect him from the jostling crowd and signalled to the driver to bring up the Land Rover. The professor jumped into the car, followed by Kabwa.

'Take me with you, Professor, you've seen how useful I can be. You said so yourself, I'm the crutch of your old age. Take me with you and enrol me in a good school, a school for Whites, and when you go dig up your old bones, I'll be with you to protect you from the evils of the living and the dead.'

'Kabwa, you're a good boy, and I want to do something for you. I already told you: Dorothée, who is staying in Astrida, will take care of you. You'll go back to school and when I return, I'll take you onto my team, I promise.'

'Thank you, Professor, Sir, I'll wait for you, don't forget me. Don't forget your crutch.'

The assistants and the students had finally climbed into the Land Rover. The car was just starting forward when they saw the councillor waving frantically at them. The driver stopped short and the councillor gripped the door:

'Mister Professor, Sir, all these good people who have drunk in your honour, you have to pay for their Primus, you almost forgot! They did this for you, out of respect for you, they came here in your honour, and they're poor. Look, I have the little bill here. It has been a great honour for them as for me to have you among us.'

The professor read the little bill, smiled, took a few banknotes from his wallet, and said:

'Very well, and here's so that your good people can drink to my health some more and not forget me. I'll be back.'

It was with great relief that they watched the professor and his retinue leave. 'What were those Bazungu doing here on our hillside?' everyone wondered. 'Measuring the trunks of old pagan trees, going up the mountain that no one should climb, gathering up old bones . . . And all this to call down on us the vengeance of the spirits and the anger of the padri, who look poorly on these new Whites.' And the catechist added, as he'd heard from the missionaries' own mouths: 'Did that professor, filled like so many others with false science, believe he could revive the old paganism and its gory rituals?' The catechist was especially peeved at Gasana: where had he come up with that story just to make the professor happy, how had he made up all those lies that did such injustice to Rwanda, that made our ancestors out to be savages even worse than the ones in America? And all that for a few ten-franc notes, Judas's pieces of silver that Gasana had gladly received.

He should repent and swear on the cross, on the medallion of Maria, on the mwami, on our Rwanda, on his children and his children's children that everything he'd told the professor was nothing but falsehoods born from his own avarice or from debility caused by his extreme old age. The councillor would put his confession in writing and it would be sent to the Administrator and the chief, who would no doubt deem it wise for the honour of his chiefdom to make sure the disavowal, duly signed by Gasana's thumb and index prints, reached the professors in Astrida who studied the history of Rwanda and its races seriously.

Gasana's face lit up in a large toothless grin:

'You need stories for every kind of ear. If the padri asked me for some seasoned to their taste, I would serve them just as many. Don't be angry. And besides, there's nothing you can do against my words. They won't just vanish like the ones in the tales. They won't dissolve in the hazy memories of children. They are already far away. They will cross the oceans. They will remain written down in the professor's book like the words of Jesus in your Gospels. They might be in the language of the Bazungu and I don't know if it will still be my story but the professor told me: my name will be in his book. I, Gasana, son of Gatera, of Kagango, of Kiromba, of Gafuku, of Ntorezo, of . . .'

'That'll do, Gasana, leave your ancestors be, you'll be joining them in Hell soon enough, like the old pagan you are.'

But many were also annoyed at Kabwa for having been the old professor's little dog. They laughed at his pretensions: did he really believe the professor was going to adopt him? Him, a hoodlum, a petty thief who'd got himself expelled from school, and because of a professor, to boot? He was still the same little liar: could anyone seriously imagine him, Kabwa, who was so black, with such a white papa? They chided him for guiding the professor and his team to the top of the mountain to collect old bones. Obviously this could unleash the ire of the dead, who have nothing better to do than torment the living. Gatwa and Gahene thought Kabwa had gone to Astrida. He would be staying, he'd told them, with the professor's female assistant while waiting for his supposed new father to return. He had also bragged that someday he might marry that young lady, who, even though she was no great beauty by Rwandan standards nor exactly in the first blush of youth, was undeniably all white. Gatwa and Gahene, trembling with envy, swore they'd go to Astrida, to Usumbura, to the ends of the earth if necessary, and bash their ex-pal's face in.

The following Sunday, at High Mass, everyone at first listened with half an ear to the padri's sermon. 'There were,' he said, 'false prophets who told false tales. Those who heeded those false tales, and those who read them, if they knew how to read, went straight to Hell. To those bad people who told false things to the Lord's innocent little children, Yezu had promised a strange punishment: an urusyo would be attached around their neck, a millstone, and they would be thrown into Lake Kivu.' Without transition, the padri asked them to pray for everyone, even for the enemies of Yezu, for those who should have been condemned to the bottom of the Kivu. And that's when he arrived at what he'd no doubt wanted to say all along: 'I have some sad news to relate: the professor who came to your hillside is dead. He was killed in an airplane accident: the small plane that connected with Sabena in Usumbura crashed in the tall mountains overlooking Lake Kivu. I've been told that the airplane got caught in a fierce storm, that it was struck by lightning, and that the airplane broke into a million pieces. Let us pray for the professor and for those who were travelling with him. The professor is surely in need of our prayers. But God is merciful: they say that the prayers of the Lord's innocent little children can lessen for an instant the sufferings of the damned.'

When the cloud of dust raised by the motorcycle had settled, the catechist commented on the padri's sermon for those who had remained to chat on the packed-earth churchyard in front of the outpost.

'Did you fully understand what the padri said? Did you fully understand Yezu's punishment? The wicked shall be tossed to the bottom of the lake with a millstone around their necks, as they once did for the adulteress. And who, then, were those wicked? False scientists who had not gone to the mission school but to the devil's school. Yes, the padri have told me: there are devil's schools where they come from. And these false scientists mislead little children with their big words that no one under-stands. They try to push them back into worshipping the old fetishes, the trees, the sheep. Well, here, too, on our hillside, the professor came to mislead us and restore the time of the pagans. You heard him yourselves: he wanted to rebuild Akayezu and Mukamwezi's hut, destroy the statue of Maria that the monsignor of Kabgayi gave us. He wanted to sacrifice children to Kibogo on our mountain.

'But you have also heard: his airplane was struck by Yezu's fury. You must fear Yezu's fury. And so, to thank him for having saved us from the snares of the wicked, let us pledge here and now to erect a great cross on the top of Mount Runani. It will protect us from every demon, from Kibogo and all the spirits of Hell.'

A murmur from the gathering, which the catechist took as assent, greeted the end of his speech.

But late at night, when the hearth fire was no more than a dome of glowing embers, the spinners of tales asked:

'And why should we attribute this vengeance to Yezu? Didn't Kibogo also have reason to complain of this professor? What was that professor doing up there on Kibogo's mountain? Stealing the remains of the woman who had been his bride? As for us, we shall recount how Kibogo came down in his cloud, followed by the endless train of his brides who, for centuries and centuries, nourished his umuzimu in the chapel of the king's palace, of intore dancers with their lion's manes, of his countless herds of cattle with their long horns. Kibogo struck with his Thunder-Spear the thieves of bones, the thieves of memory. And he took back the bones of his bride, who immediately became again the young girl of unequalled beauty she had once been, and she regained pride of place among those who had been promised to him. In our tales, Kibogo too can shake the sky and set off the thunder: isn't the tale of Kibogo equal to the tale of Yezu?'

And in the deepest secret of night, the storytellers spin and spin again the tale of Kibogo.

DAUNT BOOKS

Founded in 2010, Daunt Books Publishing grew out of Daunt Books, independent booksellers with shops in London and the south of England. We publish the finest writing in English and in translation, from literary fiction – novels and short stories – to narrative non-fiction, including essays and memoirs. Our modern classics list revives authors whose work has unjustly fallen out of print. In 2020 we launched Daunt Books Originals, an imprint for bold and inventive new writing.

www.dauntbookspublishing.co.uk